HOLIDAY STORIES

Enid Blyton's
HOLIDAY STORIES

h

Hodder
Children's
Books

A Catalogue record for this book is available from the British Library

ISBN 978 1 444 92388 9

Printed and bound in Great Britain by Clays Ltd, St Ives plc

The paper and board used in this book are made from wood from
responsible sources.

Hodder Children's Books
an imprint of Hachette Children's Group
Part of Hodder & Stoughton
Carmelite House, 50 Victoria Embankment
London EC4Y 0DZ
An Hachette UK company

www.hachette.co.uk

Contents

Introduction

Enid Blyton (1897–1968) wrote over six hundred books in her lifetime and remains one of the world's favourite writers for children. Best-known for her stories about the Famous Five, Secret Seven and the Naughtiest Girl, she delighted readers with outdoor adventures, picnics and fairy capers in the sunshine.

Here is a selection of some of her best summertime stories.

Enjoy the stories – and your holidays!

At Seaside Cottage

At Seaside Cottage

Part One

IT WAS summer time. The sky was blue and the sun shone down. Peter was lying on the grass with Janet beside him.

'I'm so hot I'm sure I'm going to melt,' said Peter.

'We can't take off any more of our clothes,' said Janet. 'We've only got bathing costumes on as it is!'

'I wish we were by the sea,' said Peter, rolling over on his front. 'Oh, Janet, think of it! Little waves rolling up the beach, golden sand to dig in, lots of bathing, and perhaps a boat to go sailing in!'

'Woof!' said a voice suddenly, and there came the sound of scampering feet. Then a golden spaniel flung himself on the two children, barking madly.

'Oh, Scamper! Get off my middle,' cried Janet. The dog at once jumped on to Peter, who squealed.

'Scamper! Stop licking my ear! Oh, what a wet tongue you've got. Stop kissing me, you silly dog! I shall have to get a towel in a minute!'

'Woof!' said Scamper, and licked Peter's nose instead.

Peter took hold of one of the spaniel's long ears. 'If you don't stop licking me, I won't let go your ear!' he said. 'What's made you so excited today?'

'He looks as if he has some good news for us, doesn't he?' said Janet. 'Scamper, tell us what it is!'

'Woof!' said Scamper, and shook his ear free. Then he galloped off up the garden. Peter sat up.

'What *is* the matter with him? Oh, there's Mummy. *She* looks pleased about something too. Hallo, Mummy!'

Mummy came down the garden with Scamper jumping up and down beside her. She was smiling.

'Well, children,' she said. 'I've got something nice to tell you. We're all going for a holiday by the sea!'

'*Mummy*! We were just saying how we wished we were by the sea!' said Janet.

'And we *knew* Scamper wanted to tell us some good news!' said Peter. 'When are we going?'

'Tomorrow,' said Mummy. 'So you will have to come and help me to pack at once. Granny has invited us to stay with her in her cottage at Sandy Cove.'

'Oh!' cried the children in delight, and they got up and began to run round just as madly as Scamper.

'I love Granny's cottage. The sea comes almost to her back gate,' cried Peter.

'Scamper, you've never even *seen* the sea. You'll love it.'

'Woof!' said Scamper, quite agreeing.

They all set off to the house to pack, chattering at the tops of their voices.

'I shall take my ship.'

'I'm glad my doll has a bathing costume. She'll love to wear it.'

'Woof! Woof!'

'Don't let's forget to take some balls to play with on the sand.'

'Woof!'

'Oh, Mummy, isn't it lovely? I feel so excited!'

All the packing was done by the evening. Daddy came home with the train tickets, and even Scamper had a dog-ticket. He felt very proud.

Everyone was excited the next day. Janet said she couldn't possibly eat any breakfast, so Scamper ate her sausage because Mummy said it couldn't be left in the larder. Scamper thought that was a very good beginning to a holiday – a whole sausage at once!

'Here's the taxi, quick, it's at the door!' shouted Peter suddenly. The taximan went to help Daddy with the luggage. Soon it was all in the taxi.

Daddy went all round the house to make sure that

every window was closed. Then he slammed the front door and got into the taxi with the others.

'We're off!' he said. 'No, Scamper, sit on the floor, please. You really can't sit on my knee.'

'I hope we're in time for the train,' said Peter. 'Oh, Mummy, wouldn't it be awful if we didn't catch it!'

'We could get the next one, silly,' said Janet. 'Look – here we are at the station already. Mummy, there's a train in. Oh quick, in case it's ours!'

They all got out of the taxi, and at that very moment the train began to pull slowly out of the station.

'It's all right,' said Daddy, seeing the children's alarmed faces. 'That's not our train. It's going the wrong way!'

They went into the station. It was an exciting place. A goods train came in and the children counted the trucks behind it.

'It's got thirty-four trucks to pull!' cried Peter. 'The most we've ever counted! Oh, Mummy, hadn't I better put Scamper on the lead in case he gets on the line? He will keep going to the edge of the platform.'

'Look – the signal's set to show our train is coming!' cried Janet. 'I can just see it coming. Yes, it's our train!'

So it was. It came rushing into the station, and poor Scamper was so frightened that he tried to get under a pile of luggage and hide.

'He thinks it's some kind of great big dog coming to eat him,' said Janet. 'Come on, Scamper – get in!'

They all got into an empty compartment. The children knelt up at the windows on opposite sides. Scamper got under the seat. He was still frightened.

The train began to move very slowly, and the children shouted with joy. 'We're moving! We're off to the sea!'

'Look, we can see our back garden!' cried Janet. Scamper came from under the seat and jumped up by her to look. 'See, Scamper, there is the cat next door. Wave your paw to her!'

It was great fun going in the train. There was such a lot to see from the windows. There were fields of cows, winding rivers with bridges over them, lots of back gardens, some neat and tidy, some badly-kept and full of weeds. There were dark tunnels to go through, high bridges to go over, and stations to stop at. The children couldn't think how Daddy and Mummy could sit and read when there was so much to be seen from the windows.

'Soon be there now,' said Daddy, after a long time. 'Look out for the first sight of the sea, children. You will see it after the next station.'

And so they did! Janet gave a squeal that made everyone jump. 'Oh look! I can see the sea, like a blue line over there! Look, Scamper, that's the sea!'

'Woof!' said Scamper, looking at a cat on a wall. He didn't know in the least what the sea was like.

'Next station's ours,' said Daddy, beginning to collect the bags off the rack.

The train came to a full stop at the next station, and couldn't go any further because the line ended there. The children tumbled out of the carriage excitedly. They were at the sea at last!

'There's Granny! And Grandpa! Granny, we're here!'

Granny hugged them all, and patted Scamper. 'Welcome to Sandy Cove!' she said. 'Let the porter bring the luggage. We can walk, it's so near.'

The sun shone down from a lovely blue sky. When the children turned the first corner they cried out in delight.

'The sea! Oh, look at all the sparkles on it. Grandpa, is the tide in or out?'

'Going out,' said Grandpa. 'You'll be able to dig in the sand all afternoon. Well, well, it's nice to have you here. Now I shall be able to have somebody to take me out on the big steamer. Granny won't come with me, because she's afraid of being sick!'

'We'll come, Grandpa! We'd love to,' said the children, and Scamper ran round and round them, getting in everyone's way, he was so excited.

'Oh, can we go down on the sands now, this very

minute?' asked Janet. 'They do look so lovely.'

'Wait till after dinner,' said Granny. 'I'm sure you must be very hungry. I've got a nice lunch waiting for you.'

'What is it?' said Janet, suddenly feeling hungry.

'Cold meat, salad, and potatoes in their jackets,' said Granny.

'And lots of ice cream for a pudding,' added Grandpa.

'Our very favourite dinner!' said Peter, and he rushed on ahead to Granny's little cottage.

It was a pretty one, set right by the sea. The back garden ran down to the beach, and a little white gate led on to the sands.

'Has the sea ever come into your back garden?' asked Janet.

'Oh, yes. It often does in the winter,' said Granny, pushing open her little front gate. 'Now, welcome to Seaside Cottage, all of you. I hope you will have a lovely time here.'

'We shall, we shall!' said Peter, and gave her such a hug that he almost lifted her off her feet.

Soon they were all sitting down to dinner. How hungry they were! 'I've got my seaside appetite already,' said Peter. 'I could eat my dinner all over again!'

'You can't possibly eat any more, Peter,' said Mummy. 'Now, go up to your room, both of you, and get into your shorts and sandals. Then you can go straight out on to the beach.'

It wasn't long before Peter, Janet and Scamper were running down Granny's back garden, through the little white gate, and out on to the yellow sands. They all danced about like mad things. 'We're at the seaside! Our holiday's only just beginning! Hurrah, hurrah, hurrah!'

'Woof, woof, woof!' barked Scamper at the top of his voice.

'Come down to the water and see the sea, Scamper,' said Janet. 'Come along. We'll run right down to the very edge.'

So off they all went, but when Scamper really saw the sea, stretching away blue and smooth for miles and miles, he was frightened. And when a wave ran up and caught his paw, he barked in fright.

'It's all right, Scamper. The sea won't eat you,' cried Peter. 'Come on, let's paddle.'

And in went the two children, their toes loving the feel of the warm water and soft sand. They paddled till the water came above their knees. The little waves splashed round them, and soon Scamper forgot to be afraid and came bounding in the sea after them.

'Oh, Scamper! You'll have to swim if you come out much deeper,' cried Peter. 'And we none of us have learnt to swim yet.'

'Oh, look! Scamper can swim! He's swimming beautifully. Look how he uses all his legs at once!' called Janet. 'Peter, how does he know how to swim? He hasn't had a single lesson.'

'Dogs don't need to be taught,' said Grandpa's voice, from the edge of the sea. 'But children do. You must learn while you are here, and as soon as you can both swim six strokes we'll go on the steamer!'

What fun the children had that first day! They dug a big castle, with Grandpa helping. They made a wide moat round it for the sea to fill. They decorated it with seaweed and shells. They went to buy a little flag to put on the top. It did look a lovely castle.

'Sit on it with Scamper, Janet,' said Peter. 'Let the tide come right up.'

'It won't be up till after tea,' said Grandpa. 'Look, here comes Mummy with a picnic tea.'

Tea was lovely. They all had it sitting on the sands. Scamper upset Janet's milk, and ate Granny's bun when she wasn't looking, but otherwise he was a very good dog.

'Now the tide's coming up, look,' said Grandpa. 'Go and sit on the castle with Scamper, Janet.'

So off they went, and soon Janet was proudly sitting on the very top, waving the little Union Jack, while Scamper growled fiercely every time a wave came too near. When one actually dared to touch the castle he barked very angrily indeed. 'Woof, woof! Woof, woof!'

A big wave came up and washed right round the castle. Janet gave a squeal. 'Oh, the castle is going. I felt it!'

Another wave came. Scamper barked so furiously that Granny felt quite alarmed. Then a still bigger wave came, and Janet had to stand up in case she was washed away with the castle!

'That was fun!' she said, wading back to shore. 'Come on, Scamper. Good dog! I'm sure you must have made the waves feel very frightened.'

It was lovely going to bed in the little room under the roof, at Granny's cottage.

'I like this ceiling, don't you, Janet?' said Peter. 'It's not straight like ours at home. It comes slanting down almost to the floor. Oh, I do like being here!'

Part Two

It was lovely waking up the next morning. The children could hear the sound of the sea, and they could hear the seagulls calling.

'It sounds as if they're laughing,' said Janet, jumping out of bed and going to the window. 'Get up, Peter. The sea is as blue as cornflowers!'

Grandpa gave them their first swimming lesson that day. He was very good and patient with them. He had to be quite stern with Peter, though, because he was afraid that Grandpa would let go his hold of him and drop him under the water.

'Now don't be silly! You can trust me when I say I shan't let you go under the water. Watch Janet! She is much better than you are, and you are seven, a whole year older!'

Then Peter went red, and tried harder.

'Very good,' said Grandpa. 'You are doing the arm strokes better now. My word, you'll soon be able to swim after all. Then we'll go on the steamer.'

Daddy made them run about and play ball on the sands after they had bathed, to get them nice and warm. Scamper loved that. He always fetched the ball when it ran into the water.

But sometimes he didn't want to give it back to the others. He would run off down the beach with the ball, and make the children chase him for miles.

The weather was so lovely that they had all their meals, except breakfast, out of doors. The children got brown after two days in the sun, and they ate so much that Granny really thought she had better give them five meals a day!

'Let's go shrimping this evening,' said Grandpa, and he went out and bought three shrimping nets. Then they went shrimping in the shallow sandy edge of the sea.

'I've got five at once!' cried Janet in delight.

'And I've got eight!' called Peter. 'Grandpa, did you catch any that time?'

'Only two,' said Grandpa. 'We shall soon get our baskets full!'

Granny cooked the shrimps for supper. The children ate them with brown bread and butter. They were delicious.

'I do want to go and explore the rock pools,' said Janet, one day. 'Can we, Granny?'

'Of course. But go at low tide, dear, because they get very deep at high tide,' she said.

So Peter and Janet went to the blue pools that lay between the seaweedy rocks. Peter took his boat to sail on one pool. 'Look!' he called to Janet. 'She sails beautifully!'

They climbed about all over the rocks when they had sailed Peter's boat. And suddenly Janet slipped on the seaweed!

'Help!' she cried.

But before Peter could turn round, she had slid backwards into a deep pool. Splash! In she went, and the water went right over her head as she sat down in the pool.

Peter dragged her up, gasping and choking. She began to cry.

'Don't cry,' said Peter. 'Let's go back and tell Mummy all about it.'

He took Janet back to Mummy. Daddy laughed when Janet told him what had happened. And then Janet began to laugh too.

'I expect I looked funny,' she said.

Then suddenly Peter looked alarmed. 'My boat! We left it on the pond! Oh, I do hope nobody has taken it. I wonder if I shall know which pool it is.'

He ran off to get his boat. But soon he was back, looking very upset. 'I can't find my boat. It's gone. Somebody must have taken it.'

'Look! What's Scamper got?' said Mummy suddenly. They all looked round. Scamper was trotting towards them from the rock pools, and in his mouth he had Peter's boat!

'Oh, you clever dog!' cried Peter in delight. 'You

found it for me. Scamper, you're the best dog in the world. Can I buy him an ice-cream, Mummy? He does so love them.'

So Scamper had an ice-cream all to himself.

Another day, Grandpa gave Daddy and the two children a great treat. He paid Jock the fisherman to take them out in his fishing-boat to fish!

Jock's boat had a sail. It was a red one and looked lovely against the blue sky. Jock took down his sail and threw out the anchor when they were far enough out.

'Now here's where we'll get plenty of fish,' he said. 'Here's a line for you, Peter, and one for you, Janet.'

Janet caught two fish, and Peter caught three. Grandpa caught six, and Jock caught eight.

'A very fine afternoon's work,' said Jock with a grin that showed all his white teeth. 'Now, up with the sail and we'll be off back to the shore. You'll have some nice fried fish for your supper tonight!'

The wind filled the red sail, and the boat sped back

to Sandy Cove. Janet and Peter each had a turn at the tiller. They felt very grand to be able to hold the little boat on her course.

'When I'm grown up I shall have a boat just like this for my own,' said Peter.

'What will you call her?' asked Janet. 'Jock's boat is called *Saucy Sue*.'

'Then I'll call mine *Cheeky Janet*, after you,' said Peter, and that made everyone laugh.

As they came near the shore Peter saw the high cliffs farther along the cove.

'Are there any caves there?' he asked Jock.

'What? Along there in those cliffs?' said Jock. 'Oh yes. Plenty of them. You should go and explore them, but mind you do it when the tide's out or you'll get caught inside. The water comes right up to them round along there.'

'Oh Daddy – can Janet and I go and explore the caves tomorrow?' asked Peter. 'Do say yes! We might find some smugglers' caves. Mightn't we, Jock?'

'Well, there's no knowing,' said Jock, his bright blue eyes twinkling at them. 'They do say there were smugglers here a hundred years ago.'

The very next day Peter and Janet set off to explore the caves. They took Scamper with them, of course, and he raced along beside them, barking at any gull that dared to come and walk on the beach.

It was quite a long way round the cove to the cliffs where the caves were. The first cave was small and low. The next one was bigger but it didn't go very far into the cliff. But the next cave looked a likely one. It ran right back into the cliff and had a very sandy floor, clean and smooth. Peter had brought his torch with him and he switched it on.

'Look, Janet! There's an archway here at the back of this cave, and I do believe it goes right back into another cave. Let's go, shall we?'

So they went through the archway and came into another cave, very dark and seaweedy.

'Let's play here,' said Peter. 'We could be smugglers!'

Scamper dashed in and out excitedly, dragging a long bit of seaweed behind him. The children explored the second cave and then, to their great delight, they found that rough steps in the back cave led upwards into a third cave.

'This *is* exciting!' cried Peter, climbing up, his torch throwing a bright light before him.

The third cave was small and rather smelly. The children explored it thoroughly, but they could not find anything there that they thought had anything to do with smugglers.

'We've been here a long time,' said Janet. 'And do listen to Scamper barking down there in the other cave. What's the matter with him?'

They soon knew! The tide had come right up to the first cave and was splashing inside. They were caught. They stood staring out at the great, heaving stretch of blue sea, full of dismay.

'*Now* what shall we do?' said Peter.

Suddenly Scamper splashed into the waves and swam off valiantly. 'I do believe he's gone to fetch help,' said Janet, almost crying. 'Oh, I do hope he has!'

Scamper had. He swam right round the cliffs till he came to the sandy beach. Then he bounded along to Seaside Cottage. He barked and barked, and tried to drag Daddy out of the door.

'The children are in danger!' said Mummy suddenly. 'That's what Scamper has come to say. They've gone to those caves and been caught by the tide. Oh dear!'

'Now don't worry, my dear. I'll get Jock's boat and he and I will go get the children,' said Daddy. So off he went and very soon he, Jock and Scamper were rowing round the cliffs to the cave where the children stood, alone and frightened. Scamper barked to them.

Daddy and Jock got the children into the boat. Scamper licked them madly. He was so pleased to have saved them. Janet hugged him.

'Darling Scamper! Daddy, isn't he wonderful? He knew we were in danger and he fetched you.'

Daddy had a few words to say about foolish children who didn't remember the tides. 'And you especially, Peter, ought to have been more careful,' he said, 'because a brother must always look after his sister. I don't feel very pleased with you.'

But everyone was pleased with Scamper, and you should have seen the dinner Granny put down for him that night.

Part Three

Before two weeks had gone by Peter and Janet could both swim six strokes. Grandpa was very proud of them both.

'Now, I must keep my word and let you take me on the steamer,' he said. 'Shall we go this afternoon?'

'Oh yes!' cried the children. So that afternoon they walked to the little pier where small red steamers came six times a day.

'There comes the steamer now!' cried Peter in excitement. 'Look, Grandpa. It's puffing away like anything. Will it turn round at the pier?'

'She will turn before she arrives at the pier,' said Grandpa, 'and back up against it, till she's sideways on.'

They got their tickets and went to wait for the little red steamer. Before they could get on, a lot of people got off. Then Grandpa, Peter and Janet all went on board with the other people who were waiting.

'Oh, it's a lovely steamer!' cried Peter, exploring every corner. 'Look, Janet, you can even go downstairs in it.'

'Yes, that goes down to the cabin,' said Grandpa. 'In case it rains, you know. But it won't rain, so we'll sit up here on deck. Come along.'

What fun it was when the steamer started off. It gave a deep hoot that made the children jump, and then set off quite fast over the sea.

'It's going to Pride Bay!' said Peter. 'That's a big place, isn't it, Grandpa? Is it as nice as Sandy Cove?'

'Well, you'll see,' said Grandpa. 'Now look how small our little pier is. We've come quite a long way already.'

'It's very windy, isn't it?' said Janet.

'Oh, isn't the sea blue? Look, Grandpa, is that Pride Bay far away over there? It looks so very small.'

But it didn't look small when they got to it. It was a big seaside town. The beach was so crowded with people that the children could hardly see any sand. There was a lot of noise, too, bands playing, men shouting and children yelling.

'I don't like this,' said Janet. 'It's too big and noisy, and isn't the beach dirty? I like Sandy Cove best, Grandpa. Shall we just have an ice-cream somewhere and catch the next steamer back? It's the steamer-ride I like, not the place we've come to!'

'That's just what *I* feel!' said Grandpa, looking quite pleased. 'Sandy Cove for me every time. Look, we'll go and get an ice-cream over there, up on the cliff, and we can watch for the next steamer to come.'

So they had an ice-cream up on the cliff, where it was windy and fresh. Pride Bay was a beautiful bay, blue and calm. It was fun to watch the little red steamer they had come on, go puffing away, and another one come to meet it from somewhere up the coast.

They went down to the crowded beach to get to the pier. Pierrots were playing and singing to the people. Ice-cream men did a fine trade. A string of little donkeys stood patiently waiting for riders.

'Let's have just one ride!' said Peter.

So they had a ride, and even Grandpa did too. The three donkeys galloped along the sands and back again. Then it was time to go to the pier to wait for the little red steamer.

It was lovely to arrive back at Sandy Cove again. Granny, Mummy, Daddy and Scamper were at the little pier to meet them. Scamper flung himself at them as if he hadn't seen them for a whole year!

'It was a lovely trip, said Janet, 'but we *are* glad to come back to Sandy Cove. It's the nicest seaside place there is!'

'It's a pity we've ever got to leave it,' said Peter. 'Oh Mummy, is our holiday soon coming to an end? I shall be so sad if it is.'

'I'm afraid it is,' said Mummy. 'We must go the day after tomorrow.'

'Oh dear! Not so soon as that!' cried Janet. 'Oh Mummy, we must collect heaps of shells, and some ribbon seaweed too, to take back – and can we take some crabs?'

'Oh no,' said Mummy. 'Not crabs. They wouldn't live away from the sea. But you can hunt for shells and take some nice seaweed back, if you like.'

'Only one more whole day,' said Janet, as they got into bed that night. 'Isn't it sad, Peter? Why do lovely holidays like this go so quickly?'

'We must do simply *everything* tomorrow,' said Peter. 'We must dig, and paddle, and bathe, and shrimp, and go out in Jock's boat. It's the last chance we'll have!'

So on that last day the two children were very busy. They dug an enormous castle with a moat that ran down to the sea.

They paddled with Scamper and they bathed with him. Janet swam eight strokes and Peter swam nine.

They went out in Jock's boat for an hour and saw him take up some of his lobster pots with lobsters in them.

They went to the rock pools and sailed Peter's boat – but this time they brought it safely back with them!

They got their fishing nets and shrimped when the tide was low, and they caught more shrimps than ever before. They found a box for shells and filled it. And they both found a beautiful long piece of ribbon seaweed to take home and hang up to tell the weather.

'When it's dry you'll know the weather will be fine. When it's wet, the weather will be rainy or cloudy,' said Granny.

* * *

At last the time came to go. Granny and Grandpa went to see them off in the train. Scamper was sad too, and he put his tail right down.

'I don't like letting you go, said Granny. 'I really don't. I don't know what I shall do without you all.'

'I shall only let them go if they promise me something,' said Grandpa suddenly.

'What?' asked the children.

'Promise me you'll come back next year in the summer holidays,' said Grandpa. 'Do you promise?'

'Oh *yes*, of *course* we promise!' cried the children, as the guard waved his flag.

'We'll come back next year. Goodbye, Granny; goodbye, Grandpa; goodbye, Sandy Cove!'

The Magic
Ice Cream

The Magic Ice Cream

ONCE, WHEN Tick and Tock, the two brownies, were sitting in their garden enjoying two strawberry ice creams they had just bought, a witch came by. As she passed, the tip of her cloak blew up and touched Tock's ice cream.

He grew red with excitement. 'Did you see that?' he said to Tick. 'That's made my ice cream a wishing ice! Whatever I wish will come true! Oh my, oh my, what luck!'

'I wish for six ice creams!' said Tick, at once. Immediately six lovely ice creams appeared on the table. Tock stared at them in surprise and anger.

'Tick! You're not to use my wishes. This is my magic ice, not yours. I wish all those six ices away!'

At once the ices disappeared, before Tick had even eaten a mouthful of them. He was very angry.

'Mean thing!' he shouted. 'I'd let you share my wishes if I had any! I wish for my ices to come back!'

At once they all appeared again and Tick started eating one.

'And I wish them all away!' yelled Tock, in a temper. Off they went, in a twink.

'I wish you had a strawberry ice down your neck!' Tick shouted angrily.

'Ooh! Ah! Ooh!' Tock squealed as a large strawberry ice suddenly squeezed itself down his neck. 'You horrid thing, Tick! I wish you had some hot cocoa down your back!'

Then it was Tick's turn to squeal as hot cocoa trickled down his back and burned him.

'Stop it, Tock, stop it burning me!' he begged. Tock laughed loudly when he saw Tick wriggling about, and that made Tick very angry.

'I wish you had no shoes on and had to walk on prickly hedgehogs!' he cried. Oh dear – poor Tock! At once his shoes flew off and he found himself walking on a hundred prickly hedgehogs, which squealed and ran about. Tock at once wished them away again, but his feet were very much pricked and scratched. He glared at Tick, who began to look frightened, afraid of what Tock would wish for him.

'Listen, Tock, listen,' he said, quickly. 'This is silly of us. We are wasting good wishes. Let us wish for good things, things we really want, instead of teasing each other like this.'

'I've a good mind to wish you at the bottom of the sea!' grumbled Tock, sitting down and putting on his shoes.

'Oh no, Tock, *dear* Tock, don't do such a dreadful thing as that!' begged Tick. 'Remember, we are brothers and we live together and are fond of one another.'

'Well, don't you keep wishing then, because this is

my magic ice, and not yours,' Tock said sulkily. 'I shall wish the wishes for both of us. You're not to wish at all. Do you hear?'

'Very well, Tock,' said Tick. 'Tell me when I may choose a wish, please.'

'I am going to wish a wish for myself first,' said Tock. He thought for a minute. 'I wish for a very fine suit of gold,' he said. At once his tunic, stockings, shoes and hat changed into gleaming gold, and Tick cried out at the sight of him.

'You look just like a prince, Tock!' he cried. 'Wish for a suit like that for me.'

'I wish Tick a very fine suit of silver,' said Tock, who didn't wish Tick to be quite so fine as himself. Tick was disappointed and sulked.

'And now I wish for a fine horse!' said Tock. At once a beautiful black horse cantered into the garden. Tock was rather frightened.

'Ooh!' said Tick, surprised. 'Wish me one like that, Tock!'

But Tock wasn't going to let Tick be as grand as he was. Oh no! 'I wish a fine donkey for Tick!' he cried. A little grey donkey trotted up to Tick, but he cried out in rage.

'Tock! You mean thing! You've only wished me a suit of silver, instead of gold, and now you've got me a donkey instead of a horse. I wish them all away!'

Off went the horse and the donkey and away went the suits of gold and silver! Tock stared at Tick in a great rage. Then he rushed at him and hit him on the nose.

Tick cried out with pain and rushed at Tock. He knocked him over and Tock banged his head against the leg of a garden chair. He sat up and began to cry. Tick cried too, for his nose began to bleed.

'My n-n-n-nose is b-b-bleeding!' he sobbed.

'And I've a fearful b-b-b-bump!' wept Tock.

'Let's go indoors and bathe your nose and my bump, Tick.'

So in they went, sorry for themselves and beginning

to feel sorry for each other. Tock sponged Tick's nose and Tick sponged Tock's bruise.

'Let's not quarrel, Tick,' said Tock. 'We've wasted all those wishes, you know. They've gone.'

'I won't quarrel any more,' wept Tick. 'Let's be kind and generous, Tock, and not spoil things for one another. As soon as we get outside, you wish for something nice for yourself, and I promise I won't spoil it.'

'No – I'll wish for something lovely for you!' said Tock, generously.

They went outside and sat down to think what lovely things to wish for – and then Tock saw a dreadful thing. While they had been indoors, the sun had melted the magic ice cream, and the next-door cat was licking it up! Imagine it! Licking up an enchanted ice cream! Tock drove the cat away – but it was too late. There was no ice cream left.

So it wasn't any good wishing. The ice cream was gone and the magic with it. It was very sad, very upsetting. Tock cried big tears and so did Tick.

'All we've g-g-got is a hurt n-n-nose and a b-b-bumped head!' sobbed Tock.

'Never mind, Tock,' said Tick, putting his arms round the other brownie. 'We'll know better next time.'

'There won't be a n-n-next time!' wept poor Tock. 'We shall never have such a ch-ch-chance again!'

And you know, I'm very much afraid they never will!

Wagger Goes
to the Show

Wagger Goes
to the Show

'MUMMY, THERE'S to be a garden-party at the Hall, in the grounds, next month!' said Terry, coming in with his sister Alice and his dog Wagger. 'Can we go?'

'There's to be all kinds of fun,' said Alice. 'There's a donkey to give rides, and all sorts of competitions, and swings and ice-creams. We can go, can't we, Mummy?'

'Yes, of course,' said Mummy. 'You must start saving up your money at once, then you will have a nice lot to spend.'

'And, Mummy, there's a baby-show,' said Alice.

'Isn't it a pity we haven't got a baby, because then it might win a prize at the baby-show. I expect Mrs Brown's baby will win. It's the fattest baby I ever saw.'

'Oh, it isn't always the fattest babies that are the best ones,' said Mummy. 'Well, I'm afraid you can't take a baby. You're my baby, Alice, and you're seven!'

'Let's put Alice in for the baby-show,' said Terry with a grin.

'I'm not a baby,' she said. 'Oh, there's a dog-show too. We're going to put Wagger in for that. What sort of dog is he, Mummy?'

'He's what we call a mongrel – just a mix-up of a dog. He's not pure-bred like the fox-terrier next door. He's a very ordinary, rather ugly mongrel.'

'Mummy!' said both children in horror. 'He's *not* ugly! He's beautiful.'

'Well, darlings, you think he's beautiful because he's yours and you love him,' said Mummy. 'But he isn't really beautiful. His tail is too long. He's too big. His ears aren't quite right. He'd never win a prize at a dog-show.' Wagger looked up at the children and wagged his long plumy tail. They stared down at him, looking into his bright eyes.

'I didn't know he was a mongrel,' said Alice. 'I didn't know he was a mix-up dog. I thought he was the nicest dog I ever knew. I still think so.'

'So do I,' said Terry and he gave Wagger a stroke on his head. 'And I'm going to take him to the garden-party even if all the dogs there turn up their noses at him! He'd hate to be left behind.'

'Well, don't put him into the dog-show,' said Mummy. 'Everyone would laugh at him, he's such a peculiar-looking dog. Yes, I know he's a darling, and faithful and loving – but he *is* ugly!'

The children went out, with Wagger jumping beside them. They simply couldn't see that he was ugly at all. 'He's got the nicest eyes!' said Terry.

'And the loveliest ways,' said Alice. 'Does it matter

so much that he's a mongrel? Oh dear – it's a shame he can't go in for the show.'

'Well, he may not be the most beautiful dog, but he's the happiest and healthiest,' said Terry. 'We look after him much better than they look after their dog next door.'

'Yes, we do,' said Alice. 'Wagger always has good meals and fresh water every day. And we bath him properly, and brush his coat well every morning. And he has a warm blanket in his basket, and lots and lots of walks all the year round.'

'Wuff,' said Wagger, licking Alice's hand.

'He understands every word we say,' said Alice, and she hugged him. He licked her face all over.

'Don't be upset because Mummy said you were ugly,' said Alice. '*We* think you're lovely, Wagger.'

'Wuff,' said Wagger happily. He wagged his long tail so fast that it could hardly be seen.

The children saved up their money that month. They ran errands and weeded the garden, and cleaned

Daddy's bicycle, and whatever they were paid they put into their moneyboxes. Soon they had quite a lot of money.

'It's the garden-party tomorrow,' said Alice to Terry one day. 'Mummy's washed my blue dress for me. And you've got new jeans to wear.'

'We ought to make Wagger look nice too,' said Terry. 'Let's give him a bath with plenty of soap and warm water. And we'll brush his coat till it shines.'

'I wish we could clean his teeth too,' said Alice.

'His teeth always look white and clean,' said Terry. 'He wouldn't like you to do that. I wish we had a new collar for him. His is old and rather dirty-looking.'

'Well, that won't matter,' said Mummy. 'He's not going in for the dog-show, so he doesn't need to be all dressed up in new collars and ribbons. So long as he is clean and healthy, that's all that matters when you take him out with you. Get out the big plastic bowl if you want to wash him.'

They bathed Wagger between them. He was as

good as gold. He never made a fuss about being washed like the dog next door did. He just stood in the warm water and let himself be soaped all over. He even shut his eyes so that the soap wouldn't get into them. He was as clever as that!

The children rinsed him and dried him. Then they took turns at brushing his thick, silky coat. It was rather curly, and it was fun to see the curls come up under the brush.

They even brushed his big ears and his long tail. He looked very fine indeed when they had finished with him. He capered about in delight, barking.

'I still think he's beautiful,' said Alice, looking at him. 'He's such a happy-looking dog. His eyes are so bright, and his tail is so waggy. Wagger, you're a darling!' Wagger licked her and pranced off again. He was certainly a very lively dog, always ready for a walk or a game.

Next day the children set off to the garden-party, with Wagger at their heels, freshly brushed. They paid their money at the gate and ran beside the donkey all the way round the garden and back.

Then they had ice-creams, and Wagger licked up all the bits that dropped on the ground. After that they went to have a swing, and Wagger waited on the ground below, because he didn't like swinging.

Then they all went to see the babies at the show, and Alice was glad she wasn't the judge, because she thought all the babies were as nice as one another. Terry didn't like them so much. He said they made too much noise, and their faces were ugly when they screwed them up to cry.

Then they had another ice-cream each, and spent some money trying to fish prizes out of a pretend fish-pond with a little fishing rod. But they weren't lucky, and couldn't hook a single prize! Wagger watched solemnly, and once he wuffed as if to say 'I'm sure *I* could hook a prize if I had a chance!'

Then a bell rang, and someone called out that the dog-show was about to begin. Everyone with dogs hurried to the big tent. What fine dogs there were, to be sure. Terriers dancing about on neat little legs, Pekes, with their snub noses, looking rather haughtily around. Scotties and Sealyhams barking loudly with excitement. Really, it was all very thrilling!

'We'll go in and see the show,' said Terry. 'But we'd better leave Wagger outside, as we can't show him. It's a shame! Poor Wagger. He can't help being a mongrel.'

They tied Wagger up outside the tent and went in. There was a ring of sawdust inside, and here people walked their dogs round and round when they were showing them. The children watched, and the judges, sitting nearby, made notes and talked in low voices to each other.

Then they called out which dogs won the first prize and second prize. The fox-terrier who belonged to the family next door won second prize and got a red ticket. His owner, a big boy called Ray, was delighted.

'See, Terry,' he said, as he passed him. 'I've

got second prize for Nobby. Pity your dog's such an awful mongrel!'

Then one of the judges got up to speak. 'We have now awarded all the prizes for the various breeds of dog,' he said. 'But there is one special prize to come, for which any dog can be entered, whatever breed he is. This is a prize given for the best-kept and healthiest dog. Please bring your entries to the ring one by one.'

So one by one the dogs were all brought up. Ray brought his Nobby too, proudly wearing the red ticket marked 'SECOND' in his collar.

And then a dog walked into the ring all by himself! The children gasped. It was Wagger! Somehow he must have wriggled himself free and come to find Alice and Terry. He walked into the ring of sawdust, looking all round for them.

The judges thought he was entered for the competition. One put his hand on Wagger's collar and looked at his teeth. Wagger didn't mind at all. He just wagged his tail hard.

The judges ran their hands over his coat. They looked at Wagger's eyes. They lifted up his feet and felt down his legs. Wagger barked joyfully. He thought they were making a nice fuss of him.

Wagger was the last dog in the ring. One of the judges looked round the tent and called out loudly:

'Who owns this dog? Will they please come forward?'

Rather scared, Alice and Terry went into the ring. Wagger greeted them with loud barks, licks and jumps.

'We – we didn't mean...' began Alice. But the judge interrupted her.

'Ah, so you own this lovely dog,' he said. 'Well, I am pleased to say that we shall award him the prize for being the healthiest and best-kept dog in the show. His coat, his teeth, his spirits are all first-class – a very fine specimen of a dog, and most intelligent.'

And, to the children's enormous surprise, one judge handed Terry a white ticket marked 'FIRST' in big letters, and another judge handed Alice a new collar for Wagger, and a big box of chocolates for both of them.

'Oh, thank you,' said the children, and Terry said, 'But – he's only a mongrel, you know.'

'Any dog can enter for this kind of competition,' said the judge, smiling. 'It's for the best-kept, healthiest dog – no matter what kind he is, pure-bred or mongrel. You deserve the prize for keeping your dog in such good condition.'

Wagger barked and licked the judge's hand. The children turned away in delight, and bumped into Ray, who was holding Nobby on a lead.

'We've got a First,' said Terry, beaming. 'Oh, Ray – Wagger's got a First, and Nobby's only got a Second. I've never had such a surprise in my life.'

'Let's go home now,' said Alice. 'I want to tell Mummy. Let's go quickly. And we'll give Mummy the box of chocolates, because it was she who taught us to keep Wagger so well and happy.'

So they left the garden-party and tore home to tell Mummy the good news. She was just as surprised and delighted as they were. She hugged them all, Wagger too.

'We must all share the chocolates,' she said. 'Wagger, you look fine in your new collar. Really, you look beautiful!'

'He does, he does!' said Terry. 'And he's going to have his share of the chocolates, just for once. Three cheers for old Wagger, the best dog in the show!'

'Wuff, wuff, wuff!' said Wagger, three times, and made everyone laugh. Really, he's a very clever dog, indeed!

A Surprise
for Jimmy

A Surprise for Jimmy

JIMMY AWOKE feeling miserable, and he remembered why as soon as he had opened his eyes. It was the school treat and all the children in his class were going down to the seaside for the day.

Jimmy wasn't going. It cost five pounds to go, and his mother said she couldn't possibly pay all that just for a day. Wasn't that a pity? Jimmy looked at the blue sky outside the window and sighed. It was very sunny, with hardly a cloud in the sky. It would be glorious at the seaside.

He went down to breakfast, and afterwards his mother sent him out shopping. As he went down the street he saw an old lady hurrying to catch a bus.

Jimmy saw something fall out of her pocket as she ran. He ran too, then, and picked it up. It was her purse!

'Hey!' called Jimmy. 'Hey! You've dropped your purse!'

But the old lady didn't hear him. She clambered onto the bus and away it went, rumbling down the street.

Jimmy looked into the purse. Oh, what a lot of money there was! Wouldn't the old lady be upset when she found that she had lost her purse!

Jimmy looked round for a policeman. He thought he would tell him about it and see what ought to be done. But there was no policemen there.

Jimmy saw another bus coming, and he had an idea. He would get into this bus and go after the old lady. Perhaps he could catch up with her. He would watch the bus in front and see when she got out.

He jumped into the bus and off they went. It

was a fast bus and very soon it was not far behind the other bus. Jimmy sat in the front seat and watched to see if the old lady would get out. On they came to the station. Jimmy saw the old lady get out and hurry into the station. Off he jumped too and looked around.

He couldn't see his old lady! Where had she gone? She wasn't buying her ticket anywhere. Perhaps she had it already and had gone to the train.

Jimmy ran through the booking-office, and looked up and down the platforms. There she was! He saw the old lady walking on to the opposite platform from the bridge that crossed over the line. And, oh dear, there was a train coming in! Would he have time to catch the lady before she went?

Over the bridge he raced and down to the platform. The train was at a standstill there. Jimmy saw that it was a corridor train, with a passage all the way through it from one end to the other, through the carriages. He opened a door and jumped into the passage. Then he began to look into every compartment to find the old lady.

And oh my goodness me, suddenly a whistle blew, and the train started off! Jimmy couldn't open the door in time, and there he was, being carried away by the train! What a dreadful thing! And he hadn't a ticket!

Jimmy stood in the passage and felt frightened. Where was the train going to? He wondered if he dared ask anyone.

As he was standing there, feeling very miserable, he heard a noise in the next compartment. Someone was saying, 'Oh dear, oh dear, oh dear!' in a frightened voice.

Then he heard the voice say, 'I've lost my purse! Perhaps I have dropped it on the floor. Could somebody look for me, please?'

It must be Jimmy's old lady. He forgot his own troubles, and looked into the compartment. Yes, there she was, looking very worried, and two of the other passengers were looking on the floor for the purse. Jimmy pushed back the door and went in. He held out the little black purse.

'Here it is!' he said. 'You dropped it in the street when you were running for the bus.'

'Oh, my purse, my purse!' cried the old lady gladly, and she took it from him. Then she looked very puzzled.

'But if I dropped it so far away, how did you manage to get here to me?' she asked.

'Well, you see, I got into the next bus and followed you to the station,' said Jimmy. 'And I saw you were going to catch this train, so I hopped on it to find you. And now the train has taken me with it, and I don't know what to do.'

He looked so upset that the old lady was quite upset herself.

'Never mind, never mind,' she said. 'Come and sit down by me. I'll look after you. This train is going to the seaside, you know. It doesn't stop till it gets there.

So you'll have to go to the seaside with it. But what does that matter? We'll telephone your mother to say you are all right, and you shall spend the day with me on the sands. Would you like that?'

Well, would you believe it! Here was Jimmy waking up miserable because he wasn't going to the seaside with the others – and now he was going after all, by mistake. What a very funny thing!

The old lady shared her biscuits with him on the train. When it arrived at the seaside she phoned Jimmy's mother to say he was all right and she would put him on the train for home after tea. Then off they went to the beach.

What fun they had! The old lady had three grandchildren, who met her at the station, and they took Jimmy down to the sea at once. He paddled and bathed, dug castles, and caught shrimps with a net – and then the children's mother and granny brought down a lovely lunch for them on the beach.

All afternoon they sailed ships on the pools, and

when teatime came they sat on the beach and boiled a kettle for tea. There were jam sandwiches and buns and chocolate cakes, so it was a really lovely tea.

They were all sorry when the time came to take Jimmy to the train. 'Come again!' they said. 'Come again!'

Their granny paid for his ticket, and kissed him goodbye. 'You deserved your treat,' she said. 'It was kind of you to run after me like that with my purse. You behaved like a little gentleman, and I'm glad you had a day at the sea after all!'

Next day when the school children told Jimmy they were sorry he hadn't gone to the seaside with them, he laughed.

'Oh, I went too,' he said. 'I didn't mean to go – but I went!' And that did puzzle the children!

The Twins
Get in a Fix

The Twins Get in a Fix

THE TWINS were a pair of pickles. They were staying at the seaside, and what a mischievous pair they were! They knocked down other children's sand castles, and took their pails and hid them. They borrowed their shrimping-nets without asking, and they really made the other children very angry.

'Leave our things alone!' they said. 'You are most annoying children and we won't play with you if you behave like this.'

But the twins took no notice. They always did what they liked.

Now one afternoon the bigger children decided to

make an enormous sand castle, the biggest anyone had ever built on the beach. The twins were asked if they would like to help, for such a big castle needed everyone to dig it. But that was too much like hard work for the twins! 'No, thank you,' said Jim. 'We are going shrimping.'

'We think sand castles are babyish,' said Suzie. So they went off by themselves – but they couldn't help watching that sand castle growing!

It really *was* an enormous one! It was the kind that uncles and aunts and fathers and mothers build when they all get together and borrow our spades. Kevin and Richard, Harry and John, Sara and Mary, Lucy and Fiona, all helped to dig it. The castle grew and grew, and the moat around it became wider and wider and deeper and deeper.

'Gracious!' said Kevin, stopping for a rest. 'I really shouldn't think such a big castle has ever been built before! We shall need steps to get up to the top!'

So they cut steps to go up to the top of it. It looked very grand indeed. The children were sorry when teatime came and they had to go.

'We'll all come back as soon after tea as we can,' said Lucy. 'Then we can take turns at sitting on the top when the tide comes in.'

So they hurrried home and left the big sand castle.

But, you know, as soon as they had gone those twins ran up to look at it – and they walked up the steps right to the very top!

'Oooh! Isn't it a lovely castle!' said Jim. 'Let's call it ours. Let's sit on the top.'

'Yes, let's,' said Suzie. 'The tide's coming in, and it will be fun to see it filling the moat and swishing all round the castle.'

So the twins sat on the top and watched the waves creeping nearer and nearer. How they screamed with joy when one ran into the moat and lapped all round the castle!

Just then the other children came back and they

shouted with rage when they saw Jim and Suzie on the top of their beautiful castle.

'Get down! It's ours!' they cried. 'You wouldn't help to build it and you shan't share it!'

'Well, we just *shan't* get down!' said Suzie, and she laughed. 'And if you try and pull us down we shall kick and knock the castle all to bits. So there!'

'You horrid, nasty children!' said Kevin. 'You know quite well that *we* built this castle, and *we* wanted to sit on the top when the tide came in. Get down at once!'

'Shan't! Shan't! Shan't!' sang the twins, and they made rude faces at the others. The children round the castle were very angry, but they couldn't do anything. They were so afraid that Jim and Suzie would spoil their lovely castle if they tried to pull them down.

The waves came higher and higher, and the watching children had to run back up the beach. The tide was getting high. They went back and watched their castle.

'We're the kings of the castle, we're the kings

of the castle!' sang the twins, and they waved their hands cheekily.

Now that evening the tide was really very high. Big waves swept up to the enormous castle, and lapped all round it every time. Soon the sea was surrounding it, and the waves galloped beyond the castle and up the beach. The castle seemed quite a long way out in the sea.

The twins suddenly looked behind them – and, good gracious, the shore seemed simply miles away! The other children were playing a game of catch-ball and were no longer watching them. It really seemed as if Jim and Suzie were far away, alone on a crumbling island in the middle of the big sea.

'Oh!' squealed Suzie suddenly, very frightened. 'The sea's all round! It's deep, it's deep!'

'The castle is breaking to bits – we'll be in the water!' shouted Jim.

'We'll be drowned, because we can't swim!' yelled Suzie. 'Help!'

The other children heard the twins shouting, and they looked towards the castle. 'It's breaking up and the twins will fall into the deep sea,' said Kevin.

'A jolly good thing!' said Lucy. 'Let them have a fright!'

'Well, we can't let them drown,' said Kevin. 'Where's our boat?'

It was pulled high up on the beach. Kevin and John dragged it down to the water and got into it. They rowed out to the twins, who were now half in the water, standing on what was left of the castle. A big wave came and splashed right over them from top to toe. They nearly fell over. Kevin reached them just in time.

'This jolly well serves you right!' he said as he dragged them into the boat. 'Now, before we take you back to the shore, do you promise to leave our things alone in the future – or do you want to be dropped in the sea again?'

'We promise!' sobbed the twins. So Kevin and John

rowed them to the beach, and they ran home to change their clothes, cold and hungry.

And did they keep their promise? Yes, they did, because, naughty as they were, they knew that to break a promise is a dreadful thing to do. So now they are much nicer, but they will never sit on top of any sand castle they build. I'm not surprised – are you?

The Enchanted Cloak

The Enchanted Cloak

ONCE UPON a time the Princess Peronel asked Thimble, the pixie, to make her a very special cloak.

She came to see Thimble in the middle of the night. It was very exciting for Thimble, who was in bed and fast asleep. She had to get up and put on her dressing-gown, and curtsey to the princess when she opened the door.

'Thimble, this is a secret,' whispered the princess, looking all round to make sure there was no one else there. 'I want this cloak to wear on Midsummer Night – and I have two very special spells that I want you to sew into it as you make it.'

'What spells?' asked Thimble, going red with excitement.

'One is a spell that will make me know everything as soon as I put the cloak on,' said Peronel. 'And the other is powerful magic that will grant my wishes. Here are two spells – do take care of them.'

'It will be a very magic cloak,' said Thimble. 'What do you want me to make it of?'

'I want it made of the purple twilight,' said the princess. 'That's difficult, I know – but maybe you can get some of the purple. Line it with some silver-dawn sky, will you? And sew the spells in all the time. Don't tell anyone, whatever you do!'

Thimble promised. She was very pleased to have such important work to do.

'You see, I want to wear the magic cloak on Midsummer Night, and be able to grant wishes to those pixies and fairies who deserve it,' said the princess. 'I shall know everything as soon as I put on the cloak – so I shall know which pixies deserve to have wishes given to them and which don't. It will be marvellous.'

She said goodbye and went. Thimble was so excited that she couldn't go to sleep any more that night. She took her sharpest scissors and flew up to the middle part of the eastern sky. She waited till dawn – and then she cut a silvery piece of the sky right out, folded it up, and flew down to earth again. Now she had the lining for the cloak! A cloud came to fill up the hole she had made.

She asked a brownie to get her some purple twilight, and he came back the next night with a big roll of it under his arm. It was blue-purple and very lovely.

'It's velvet,' he said. 'Did you know that the twilight was velvet? I didn't. But it is! Feel it!'

'It will make a lovely cloak,' said Thimble, feeling the thick purple velvet. 'Thank you, Brownie.'

She set to work. She cut out a marvellous cloak that would swing right out round the princess. She lined it with the silver sky, and it shone and shimmered beautifully. All the time she sewed in the two magic spells.

The spells were tiny beads – there were thousands of them! Thimble had to slip them on her needle and sew them into the lining as she worked. The cloak would be very magic when she had finished!

And then one day Wizard Sly-One looked in at the window and saw Thimble busily sewing. He knew at once that the cloak was a very special one, for he could smell magic with his nose, just as a dog can smell meat from a distance.

'Good-day, Thimble,' he said. 'What a wonderful cloak! Who is it for?'

'I shan't tell you,' said Thimble. 'Please shut the window and go away.'

'You don't talk to wizards like that!' said Sly-One, crossly.

'Yes, I do,' said Thimble, firmly. 'Go away!'

'I can smell magic in that cloak,' said the wizard, slyly. 'Will you sell it to me?'

'Certainly not,' said Thimble. 'It's for somebody else!'

'It's for the princess, isn't it?' said Sly-One, who had been told by an owl that Peronel had been to visit Thimble in the middle of the night.

'I shan't tell you a thing!' said Thimble. But, all the same, Sly-One found out. He paid a little mouse to go and listen to all that Thimble said to herself, for he knew that Thimble whispered to herself as she worked. So the mean little mouse didn't have much difficulty in finding out the secret.

Thimble whispered as she worked, 'This is for the dear princess! She wants to wear it on Midsummer Night – and then she will know everything and will be able to grant wishes. Oh, what a wonderful cloak it will be!'

The little mouse stayed under Thimble's chair and listened to all her whisperings – and then he ran off to tell Sly-One. He was paid by Sly-One, who gave him three pieces of yellow cheese. He was a horrid little mouse, but of great use to the wizard.

'Oho!' thought Sly-One. 'This is splendid! So that cloak is enchanted! Well – I must get hold of it somehow and wear it myself on Midsummer Night! Then I shall know everything – and I can wish bad things whenever I want to!'

So one spring night he crept to Thimble's little cottage and opened the window. Just beneath the sill, neatly folded, was the cloak, ready to be packed up and sent to the princess the next day. It shone curiously in the moonlight, for it really was very magic indeed.

The wizard carefully dragged the shining cloak out of the window. He shut the window – but it creaked and Thimble woke up. She gave a squeal as she saw Sly-One in the moonlight – and then she gave a much louder scream for she saw that the enchanted cloak was gone!

'You wicked fellow! Bring it back, bring it back!' shouted Thimble, jumping out of the window. But the wizard was gone. He was nowhere to be seen

– and neither was the beautiful cloak.

'And I spent so much time and trouble making it,' wept poor Thimble. 'Oh, what will the princess say?'

The princess was very worried indeed. 'Thimble, it wouldn't matter if the cloak didn't have those two spells in it,' she said. 'You see, I could do a lot of good with that cloak – but Sly-One will do bad things. How can we get it back?'

Sly-One didn't mean them to get it back. He put it away safely in a room right at the very top of his castle, in a tower that had no windows and no chimneys – only a great door that he could lock with three different keys.

Sly-One packed the cloak into a box and put the box in the middle of the room. If anyone opened the box a bell would ring, and then Sly-One would know that someone had come to get the cloak.

'But no one can get into my castle – and no one can get into that top room – and no one can open the box, for I have the key!' chuckled Sly-One. 'There it shall stay until Midsummer Night – then I will shake it out and wear it, and the magic in it will be mine. Ha, the things I will do then!'

The Princess Peronel soon found out where Sly-One had put her enchanted cloak, and she was quite in despair.

'No one, no one can get it from there!' she sighed. 'It is quite, quite impossible. Whatever shall we do? Think hard, Thimble! It's your fault that it has been stolen, you know. You shouldn't have left it so near the window!'

Thimble was just as upset as the princess. She sat and thought all day and night long, wondering what in the world could be done about the magic cloak – and then an idea came into her head. She jumped up at once.

'I can't get the cloak back,' she cried. 'But I can at least make it unwearable for Sly-One! I will have it spoilt so that he cannot wear it!'

'But Thimble, however can you do that?' asked

Peronel, in surprise. 'It's impossible! Why, we can't even get into the castle, and we certainly can't get into that top room. There are three keys to lock the door – and Sly-One has all of them tied firmly round his waist.'

'All the same, I think I know what to do,' said Thimble. 'I must call in an army of little creatures which we usually dislike, Princess – but this time they will help us.'

'What little creatures?' asked Peronel, in astonishment.

'Clothes-moths!' cried Thimble. 'Listen – we'll get hundreds of clothes-moths to creep in somewhere at Sly-One's castle. They can fly up the stairs and squeeze in through the keyholes and squash themselves under the lid and into the box where the cloak is.'

'And they can lay their eggs there!' cried Peronel, delighted. 'And the eggs will turn into grubs, who will gobble up the whole cloak, so that when Sly-One goes to put it on when Midsummer Night is here he will find there is nothing but holes!'

'Yes!' said Thimble. She clapped her hands and called out a string of magic words. In two minutes a cloud of tiny light-brown moths flew in at her window. Thimble gave her orders, and in a cloud they flew out again.

They flew to the castle. They crept in through cracks and holes here and there, under doors and windows. They flew up the winding stairs to the topmost room. They squeezed below the door and through the three keyholes – and there they were in the three-times-locked room!

They went to the big box in the middle of the floor. The lid was tight-fitting, but they found one small place where they could squeeze in – and in they all went, one by one.

Inside was the wonderful cloak. Each moth chose its own place and laid a batch of eggs. Then they all crept out again and flew off to tell Thimble that her wishes had been obeyed.

Inside the box the eggs hatched out into very tiny grubs. At once they set to work to eat the cloak. All clothes-moth grubs eat clothes of some sort – and these grubs were very hungry. How they ate! How they gobbled! They grew bigger and bigger, fatter and fatter, as they ate the cloak! Only the tiny beads they did not eat, and these fell to the bottom of the box as the grubs ate the cloak.

Midsummer Night came, and Sly-One stamped up the stairs to get out the cloak. Now, at last, he would know everything and would be able to get all his wishes granted. My, what a bad time he would give everyone!

He unlocked the door. He unlocked the box, and then he gave a cry of anger and rage. There was no cloak there!

All that was left of it was a few rags and a handful of tiny beads! The grubs had done their work well! Sly-One did not know that the clothes-moths had been there – he thought that the cloak had been stolen. In a rage he caught up the box and threw it out of the window – beads, rags, grubs and all!

The beads were scattered in the wind. The rags flew off, too. The grubs fell into the grass. The box smashed to pieces.

A small rabbit nearby saw all this in great astonishment, and ran off to tell Thimble. How delighted she was! She hurried to collect what beads she could find, for they held the magic spells, and she meant to make another cloak as soon as she could for Peronel.

She is making it now – but she hasn't quite found all the beads that got blown away by the wind. So if you find any, keep them carefully, and let her know. Her address is: Miss Thimble Pixie, Oak Tree Corner, Cuckoo Wood, near Fairyland.

I hope the second cloak won't be stolen, don't you?

Adventure
Up a Tree

Adventure Up a Tree

'HERE'S A fine tree to climb,' said Alan to John. 'Let's try this one. I should think it would rock in the wind like a ship.'

'Yes – and it doesn't look *too* difficult to get up,' said John. 'It's jolly high, Alan. We should be able to see a long way from the top.'

'Come on, then,' said Alan. 'I'll go first. I'm better than you at climbing. You follow the way I go.'

So up he went. The tree was an oak – wide-spread and very leafy. It wasn't really very difficult to climb. John followed, and soon the two boys had found a nice broad branch, not far from the top of the tree, where they could sit and eat the sandwiches they had brought.

The wind was strong. It shook the tree, and the boys liked that. 'Just like a ship swaying on the sea,' said Alan. 'I almost expect to hear the splash of the waves!'

The two boys were friends. They loved to go out together and find a hidy-hole of some kind. Today, it was a tree. They liked to take their tea, some chocolate and a book, and have a good read together.

'I've got a new adventure book,' said Alan. 'I'm in the middle of it. I'll lend it to you afterwards, John – it's really exciting!'

'I like adventure stories too,' said John. 'But I think I'd rather *have* an adventure than read about one. I've never had an adventure in my life ... I don't believe many people do – do you, Alan?'

'Oh, *yes*,' said Alan. 'And I'm sure adventures happen suddenly. Why, one might happen to us at *any* moment!'

'Pooh,' said John, staring down from the tree at the quiet countryside around. 'Whatever do you think could happen to us up here, this quiet afternooon? Nothing at all!'

'I can't really think of anything,' said Alan. 'But adventures *do* seem to happen out of nothing – at least, they do in books.'

'Is that a bird whistling?' said John, lifting his head to listen. 'I've never heard *that* song before!'

It was a flute-like whistle, rather like a blackbird's, and it sounded not very far off. Both boys listened, forgetting their talk about adventures. The whistling stopped, and then began again for a bit.

'I don't believe it's a bird,' said John. 'I think it's someone down in the wood.' As he spoke, the boys could hear twigs cracking and the rustling of leaves as somebody pushed his way through the wood below.

'Ssh!' said Alan. 'Whoever it is is coming this way. We don't want them to see us. This is our secret hidy-hole today.'

The whistling sounded again, exactly the same. 'Sounds like a kind of signal to someone,' said John. 'Somebody meeting someone, I suppose.'

'Be quiet – he's coming under our tree,' whispered Alan. Both boys sat as still as mice. Alan was right – the newcomer was now directly under their tree. Then all at once another whistle sounded. Someone else was coming, too.

'Can you see who they are?' asked John, in a whisper. 'Are they boys? Do you know them?'

Alan peered down through the branches. All he could see was the top of two heads, and each head wore a cloth cap. Then the boys heard men's voices.

'Where's Jim? He's always late! We'll wait for a few minutes, then leave a note for him.'

'Right. He'll have to know what to do, and we've got no way of getting in touch except this meeting-place. What's kept him?'

There was the sound of a match striking and then the smell of cigarette smoke. The men were evidently smoking whilst they waited.

The boys whispered together. 'We won't make a sound! The men might be angry if they knew we were over their heads.'

'All right. Don't drop your book on them, or you'll give us away. It's slipping off the branch!'

John caught his book before it fell. The men below smoked on without a word. After ten minutes or so they got up. 'I'll scribble a note,' said one, and there was the sound of rustling paper. Then there was a silence. One of them was writing.

After that the two men went, and the boys heard their voices in the distance. They looked at one another. 'It seems a bit odd, somehow,' said John. 'What shall we do? Go down and find the note?'

'Well – the third man might come and catch us,' said Alan. 'One of us would have to stay up the tree and look out for him, I think.'

'You go down, then,' said John. 'I'll stay up here. I'll whistle if I see or hear him. Buck up.'

Alan shinned quickly down the tree. He wondered if he ought to read somebody else's note – there really was something a bit peculiar about all this. The two men hadn't sounded nice men – and why should they have a meeting-place in the wood when they ought to be working?

Alan came to the foot of the tree. He looked about for the note, but there was no sign of one. That meant the men must have hidden it somewhere – in some place where the third man would know where to look for it. Alan began to hunt about.

He lifted up a big stone. Nothing there. He parted the leaves of a bush and looked in the middle. Nothing there, either. He saw a rabbit hole nearby and put his hand down. No – nothing to be found.

'How are you getting on?' called John. 'Found it?'

'No,' said Alan. 'I've looked everywhere. I'll just look round the tree-trunk – there might be a cranny somewhere.'

He was right. There was a crack in the trunk just

wide enough for him to put in his hand. He slipped it in and immediately felt paper. He drew it out. It was a single sheet torn from a notebook. Alan read what was on it.

'Bring car to l.c. gates, 3.10 sharp.'

That was all there was. What in the world did it mean? What were l.c. gates? And did 3.10 mean afternoon or early morning? Alan didn't know.

A low whistle disturbed him. 'Alan! Someone's coming!' came John's guarded voice. Alan thrust the paper back into the trunk of the oak and scrambled up the tree again. The two boys waited in silence for the newcomer.

He came straight to the tree. It must be Jim, then, whoever Jim was – the one the other two had waited for. There was the rustle of paper. Jim had known the hiding-place for it and had drawn it out. There was a moment's silence. Perhaps he was now reading the message. Then there was the rustle of paper again.

After that there was only the sound of footsteps

going away and twigs crackling on the ground now and then.

The boys slid down the tree. John asked Alan where he had seen the hidden paper, and put his hand into the crack to feel it. At once he felt paper, and drew out the same little sheet that Alan had seen.

But now a few more words had been added. 'O.K. Have arranged for us to go to Big Harry's after.'

'I don't like this,' said Alan. 'I shan't put this note back. I shall keep it. It's odd. I'll ask my father about it tonight.'

But he couldn't, because his father came home too late that night, and Alan was in bed and fast asleep. John was awake, wondering if by *any* chance they had nearly had an adventure that afternoon. It had all ended rather tamely, for both boys had had to hurry back because they were late, and had raced through the wood and through the town to their homes.

In the morning Alan's father read the newspaper as usual. He gave an exclamation. 'Well – what will happen next? Somebody set the level-crossing gates against the 3.10 train very early this morning – and when it stopped a couple of men got into the guard's van, knocked him over the head, took a mailbag and escaped. No sign of them at all!'

Alan listened, open-mouthed. The 3.10! Why, 3.10 was in that note surely? Did it refer to the train that went over the crossing in the middle of the night?

'"L.c. gates" – level-crossing gates, of course!' thought Alan. 'We might have guessed. I must tell Daddy.'

'Daddy,' he began, but his father was looking at the clock. 'Good gracious, I'm late! I shall miss my train. Goodbye, all of you!'

Alan decided to tell John before he said anything. It was Saturday, so he was free. He did the errands for his mother and then shot off to John's. He found John in a most excited state, for he, too, had seen the papers.

'I say, Alan, that note! That was the plan made for

that robbery!' began John, as soon as he saw Alan. 'I've worked it all out. They shut the gates, stopped the train, and two of them knocked out the guard and robbed the van. The third man – the one the others called Jim – brought the car to the gates, so that he might take the bag and the other two men away – to Big Harry's, wherever that might be.'

'Yes, I know!' said Alan, just as excited. 'Golly – we were in the middle of an adventure and didn't know it. We'll have to go to the police now, John. Thank goodness I've got that note, so they'll believe us.'

The police were surprised to see the two boys walking into the police station. 'Well, boys, what do you want?' said the constable there.

'We've got something to tell you about the men who robbed the train – the 3.10 last night,' said Alan.

'Tell away,' said the policeman, getting out his notebook.

'There were three of them,' said Alan, 'and one is called Jim. They had a car waiting at the gates, and they have all gone to Big Harry's.'

The policeman put down his notebook and stared in amazement at Alan. 'How do you know all this?'

'We were up a tree near where they met yesterday,' said Alan. 'They didn't know we were there. They left a note in the tree and we took it. We thought it was all very odd. I meant to tell my father but I fell asleep before he came home. Here's the note.'

The policeman whistled in surprise. He took the note and read it. He called through a door. 'Hey, come here. There are two boys who know a lot more about last night's happenings than we do!'

Soon Alan was telling his tale from beginning to end. The policemen listened. 'Go out to the tree with one of these boys and see what you can find,' the chief said to one man. 'Cigarette ends, perhaps – or footprints.'

'There *are* cigarette ends – and a match too – and footprints, but not very distinct!' said John, wishing he had been sensible enough to pick up the cigarette ends and match for himself. They were clues, of course!

'Could you boys recognise these fellows if you saw them again?' asked the chief.

They shook their heads. 'No,' said Alan. 'We only saw the tops of their heads, you see – we were up the tree. But we saw their caps, of course. They all wore cloth caps.'

'Would you know those again?' asked the chief at once.

'Oh, yes,' said Alan. 'We stared down at them for quite a long time! One had a navy blue cap with a tear in it.'

'And one had a tweed cap, awfully dirty,' said Jack. 'And the third one had a brown cap, rather new, with a big button on the top – brown and flat.'

'I want you to stay here for a few minutes,' the chief said to Alan. 'The other boy can go to the oak tree with this constable and bring back anything they find. Then we will all hop over to Big Harry's. So Big Harry knows about this, does he? Well, well – I often wondered what went on at Big Harry's!'

'What *is* Big Harry's?' asked John.

'Just a place where men can sleep for the night,' said the chief. 'It's a pity you wouldn't recognise these three again – but if you can spot their caps that will be just as good.'

John and the policeman went to the tree and collected two cigarette ends and a match. 'They smoke Silk Cut cigarettes, sir,' reported the constable, when they got back to the station. 'And this is a special kind of match, sir – rather big.'

'Right,' said the chief. 'Good. Now, you two boys, I want you to come with me and do a little cap-spotting. Ready?'

Well, it was a real thrill to go in the big police car and roar down the road to the next town. Alan and John looked at one another in delight. Whoever would have thought such a thing would happen?

They came to a narrow, rather dirty street. At one

end was a tall, ugly building. This was Big Harry's.

The police pushed their way into a dark, dirty hall. Pegs ran all the way down, hung with dirty coats and caps and hats. The chief shone a torch on to them.

'Spot the caps, boys,' he said. 'That one,' said John, pointing to a tweed one. 'And that one! That's the brown one with the flat button.'

'And here's the navy one,' said Alan. 'There you are, sir, those are the ones.'

'Thanks,' said the chief. 'Now we'll just find Big Harry and tell him to turn out all his boarders into the street. He won't know why and we shan't tell him! All we want to see is who takes those three caps. Then we shall know what to do!'

To the two boys enormous disappointment, they had to go back and wait in the police car. They didn't see Big Harry, frightened and blustering when the police told him to turn out all the men who had slept there the night before. Some were still in bed! However, they were all turned out, and, grumbling and grousing, they went to fetch their coats and caps and hats.

Of course, the three thieves took their own caps – and what a shock for them when the police arrested them and charged them with the robbery of the night before! One of them was smoking a Silk Cut cigarette, and another had a box of matches on him full of matches exactly like the one found under the tree.

'Well, boys,' said the chief, when the two boys were back at the police station, excited and thrilled. 'You did well to spot those caps! Made our job very, very easy! Those young men will not be wearing caps for a very long time. And a good thing, too.'

The boys said goodbye and left together. 'What will our parents say?' said John. 'How do you like adventures, Alan? We were in the middle of one yesterday without knowing it!'

'I like them very much – so long as I'm on the right side,' said Alan. 'I would rather catch a thief than be one. What cowards they were to attack the guard of the train like that! Gracious, John – let's have another adventure, shall we?'

'We'll look out for one,' said John. And they are looking very hard. I do hope they find another soon, don't you?

John's Hanky

John's Hanky

IT WAS very very hot. Mother told the two children that they really must put on their sun-hats when they went to play in the garden.

After dinner they sat on the hot garden-seat with their books. Alice had on her sun-hat. John had forgotten his, and he felt the sun burning his head.

'Bother!' he said to himself. 'I don't want to have to go all the way to the house to fetch my hat. I know what I'll do. I'll knot my hanky at each corner and make a nice little sun-cap of it.'

So he took out his big hanky from his pocket, and knotted it carefully in each corner. Then he set it on his head and took up his book to read.

His bookmark blew into the rosebushes after a bit, and John got up to get it. He scratched his hand badly on a rose-thorn and gave a yell.

'Ooooh! Look at that! It's bleeding like anything! I must bind it up at once.'

He put his hand into his pocket to get out his hanky. But it wasn't there, of course. He put his hand into his shirt, but he hadn't tucked it there either. He looked on the seat and on the ground. No hanky.

'Don't fidget,' said Alice. 'I'm reading.'

'Lend me your hanky then. I've hurt my hand,' said John.

Alice looked at him. Then she laughed. 'Use your own!' she said.

'I haven't got it,' said John, crossly.

'Yes, you have,' said Alice.

'No, I haven't,' said John. 'You tell me where it is, if you think I have got it with me.'

'Shan't!' said Alice, and laughed again. Then John

got cross and smacked her. She fell off the seat and yelled. She grabbed John by the knees and he fell off the seat too.

Soon they were rolling over and over on the grass, shouting and pummelling each other.

At last John sat hard on Alice.

'Now you tell me where my hanky is!' he said. 'Or I'll sit on you even harder. Have you taken it?'

'No! It's on your head, silly!' said Alice, and began to laugh again. Oh dear – so it was. John did feel foolish. He went indoors and got his sun-hat then!

The Magic
Watering Can

The Magic
Watering Can

TWEEKY WAS a lazy little pixie, who yawned all day long. He always left everything till the last possible moment, and he was always putting off till the next day the things he ought to do at once.

But there was one thing he could see he really did have to do – and that was, he would certainly have to water his garden or he was going to lose all his lettuces, his peas and his carrots! The weather had been very hot and dry, and Tweeky's garden looked like a dust heap. His lettuces were drooping, his peas were turning brown, and his carrots were so tiny that they were not worth eating.

'Bother!' said Tweeky, looking at his dry garden. 'I suppose I must water today – but what a nuisance it is, to be sure! How I hate carrying a heavy watering can to and fro, to and fro! If only I had a spell I could put into my can which would make it water the whole garden by itself!'

Now, no sooner had he thought that, than an idea popped into his head. Why not go to Mother Lucy and ask her for a spell? She probably wouldn't give him one – but she might. So off he went, three doors away, to ask her.

But she was out. There was no one in her little yellow cottage at all. Tweeky peeped inside the door and saw her neat kitchen, with all its shelves and drawers, each one labelled. He tiptoed inside and read the labels.

'Ha!' he said suddenly. 'Just look at that label – "A spell for watering cans and hosepipes, taps and hot-water jugs"! That's just what I want!'

He looked round. No one could see him – so the naughty little pixie opened the drawer, took out one of the small blue spells that were neatly lying in rows there, and hurriedly shut the drawer again. He ran out and went back to his cottage.

He looked at the spell. It was like a small lump of sugar, but blue instead of white. He knew exactly what to do with it. He fetched his can, filled it half full of water, popped the blue lump of sugar into it and shook it well, saying, 'Water, water, pour without stopping!'

Then he took the can to his lettuce-bed and tipped it up to water with it. He let go of the handle and the can stayed all by itself in the air, watering steadily, moving along the row of lettuces slowly as it did so. It was wonderful to see. It never seemed to get empty – there seemed to be a marvellous amount of water in it, and Tweeky knew it would never stop so long as the spell was in the can.

'Now I shall sit down in my garden-chair and have a nice lazy read,' said Tweeky to himself. 'That can is going to do all my work for me!'

So he sat down in his chair and began to read his book. But the sun was hot and Tweeky began to yawn. Soon he was fast asleep.

The watering can went steadily on with its work, and a splash-splash sound was heard for a long time. The can watered the lettuces, the carrots, and the peas. Then it watered the patch of grass. Then it moved to the little gravel path and watered that so thoroughly that it soon turned into a running river!

Tweeky slept soundly. The can went inside the cottage and began to water the pot-plants there. Then there really was nothing else for it to do, so it began to water the things it shouldn't!

It watered the kitchen fire and put it out with a sizzle! It watered Tweeky's bed and made it soaking wet! It poured streams of water over his dinner-table, which was still littered with dirty dishes. Goodness, what a mess it made! Then it filled the waste-paper basket full of water, and drenched all the cushions on the chairs. Gracious me, that watering can had a wonderful time, I can tell you!

Now after some time Tweeky woke up and remembered the can. He looked round to see where it was. He saw the soaked gravel path, which still looked like a stream, and he felt cross.

Wherever was that can?

Then he heard a noise of splashing inside his cottage and he jumped up in a flash. Surely that wicked watering can hadn't dared to go inside his cottage!

He rushed indoors – and oh, what a sight he saw! Everything was running with water, his fire was out, and the can was just watering Tweeky's nice new suit!

Tweeky rushed at the can, and it turned on him and watered him from head to foot! He caught hold of the handle and pulled the can to him. He put his hand into the water to get out the spell – but dear me, it had melted just like sugar! Tweeky groaned. He knew there was only one thing to do now – he must go and confess to Mother Lucy and ask her to stop the spell somehow!

He carried the can to Mother Lucy's and it poured water on his feet all the way. She was in, and she was most surprised to hear the tale that Tweeky sobbed out to her.

'Everything's spoilt – my new suit, my cushions; my fire's out, my whole house is running with water! I fell asleep, you see. Oh, Mother Lucy, I know it was very wrong to borrow that spell when you were out, but please do forgive me and help me, for I have been well punished!'

Mother Lucy blew into the can and whispered a magic word. A piece of blue sugar slowly began to appear at the bottom of the water. She slipped in her hand and took it out. At once the can stopped watering and stayed quite still.

'I won't punish you any more,' said Mother Lucy, who had a kind heart. 'I am sure you are punished enough already by having a house that is soaking wet everywhere. You will have a busy time clearing out everything, Tweeky, and drying it. My, won't you have to work hard for a long time! Well, it won't hurt you, for you have always been a lazy fellow. Perhaps this will teach you to be better in future!'

'Oh, it will, it will!' said poor Tweeky. And it certainly did! Tweeky isn't lazy any more, and he works hard every day. He has never borrowed anything again without asking, either. As for his watering can, he gave it away and bought a new one. He simply couldn't bear to see the old one sitting on the shelf, grinning at him!

Peppermint Rock

Peppermint Rock

SUE AND Robin were down at the seaside for the day. Their aunt had asked them to go, and they were very pleased indeed.

'Now, listen,' said their mother, as she put on their clean sweaters. 'I don't want you to quarrel *once* when you are at your auntie's. Not *once*. You quarrel all day long here, and I don't want Auntie Ellen to hear it.'

'It's not me that quarrels, it's Robin,' said Sue. 'He always begins it.'

'Oooh, you fibber!' said Robin. 'I would never quarrel at all if you weren't so bad-tempered and cross.'

'*Me* bad-tempered!' cried Sue. 'Well! I never heard such—'

'There you go again,' said their mother. 'You can never open your mouths without squabbling. I'll be glad to be rid of you for a day – and that's not a nice thing for a mother to have to say.'

She saw them off to the bus that took them to the sea. They squabbled all the way down, but they remembered what their mother had said, when they met their aunt. They were quite nice and polite to one another for once!

They met their big cousin Jim. They didn't like him very much, because he laughed at them.

'Hello, squabblers!' he said. 'Learnt to like one another yet? When are you going to begin quarrelling? I love to listen in to you. You're as good as the radio.'

'We don't quarrel any more,' said Sue, and Robin nodded. They had both made up their minds not to quarrel in front of big Jim, anyway!

As long as they were with their aunt or with Jim

they were polite to one another. But when they were alone – oh, what a difference!

Auntie Ellen gave them fifty pence to spend. 'Go to the shops and see what you can get,' she said. So off they went. Jim didn't go with them, but he followed them soon after.

They saw a long stick of pink-coated peppermint rock in a shop. 'Oooh, look! Peppermint rock in a great long stick!' said Sue. 'It would take ages to suck. And look, it's got "Margate" all down the middle. Even if we broke it in half, we'd still see "Margate" written in pink in the middle.'

'We'll buy a stick each,' said Robin, and into the shop they went. But the stick was fifty pence. There were no twenty-five pence ones!

'Well – you could buy this fifty pence one, and break it into two equal halves,' said the shopwoman.

So they bought the fifty pence rock, and took it out of the shop. 'I'll break it,' said Sue.

'No,' said Robin. 'I will. You won't be fair.'

He caught hold of the stick and broke it himself. He held out one piece to Sue.

'Oh, you mean thing!' she said. 'You've given me the smaller piece. You have!'

'I have not,' said Robin. '*Mine's* the smaller if anything. *I* think they're exactly the same.'

Sue snatched at Robin's and it fell to the ground. 'You horrid girl – now you've made it dusty,' said Robin. 'You be careful I don't smack you. I've not only got the smaller piece of the two, I've got the dusty one. Horrid thing!'

A voice spoke behind them. 'Aha! Two little squabblers again, I see. What's the quarrel about *this* time?'

It was big Jim. Robin scowled at him. Sue turned away. 'Go on, tell me,' said Jim. 'Maybe I can settle the matter for you.'

'Well – we bought this fifty pence rock between us,' said Sue, in a trembling voice. 'And we thought we would have half each. But Robin gave me the smaller half, the mean thing.'

'Let's see,' said Jim, and he took the two pieces to measure against each other.

'Ah,' he said. 'I think this one is a bit longer than that one. I'll soon cure that!'

And he bit a piece of Robin's rock! He chewed it up joyfully. 'Very nice. You'll enjoy it. Now let's measure it again.'

He measured – but he had bitten such a big bit of Robin's that Sue's piece was now far too long. So Jim bit a piece of hers.

'Jim! Don't! It's *our* rock!' said Sue, almost in tears. She tried to snatch her piece from Jim, but he swung it out of the way.

'Now, don't snatch. You really are a horrid pair, aren't you – quarrelling and grumbling and snatching! Let me measure again!'

'You're a meanie, Jim,' said Robin, in a rage, as Jim bit an enormous piece out of his rock. 'There's hardly any of my rock left.'

'Is that so?' said Jim, measuring again. 'My word, you're right. Sue's bit is far too long now. Well, here goes!'

And off came another bit of Sue's. The two pieces or rock were now very small indeed, hardly a mouthful each. Robin and Sue glared at Jim.

'Give us what is left at once!' shouted Robin. 'Give our bits to us!'

'Now, now – don't be so impatient,' said big Jim. 'Aren't you going to give me any payment for deciding your quarrel for you? Look, these bits are exactly the same size now – aren't I clever! What will you give me for making them right for you?'

'Nothing!' shouted Robin, in a fine temper.

'Very well, then – I'll take my own payment for my trouble,' said Jim – and do you know what he did? He popped both the last pieces into his mouth and began chewing them up.

Sue and Robin stared in despair. There was nothing to be done now. 'We'll tell your mother,' said Robin.

'She never listens to tell-tales,' said Jim. 'And she doesn't like squabblers, either. I wouldn't say anything if I were you. My word, that rock was good!' He turned and went away whistling. At the end of the road he called back to them, 'It serves you right for quarrelling about something that didn't matter!'

Well, I suppose it did – but wasn't it a horrid, disappointing thing to happen!

The Donkey
on the Sands

The Donkey
on the Sands

ALL THE children knew the little, fat, grey donkey on the sands. He used to take them for rides at a penny a time, and would trot along at a fine pace.

'I kicked him on when I had my ride this morning!' said Jim to the others one day. 'Goodness, you should have seen him gallop! He went about a mile a minute.'

'You shouldn't have done that to him,' said Nora. 'He's a dear and always does his best.'

'Pooh! You're just a silly girl,' said Jim grandly. 'You don't know how to treat horses and donkeys.

My father wears spurs when he goes riding in uniform, and when he wants to make his horse go fast he uses his spurs.'

'Well, I don't think it's right to hurt animals like that,' said Nora, 'especially things that really do their very best, like Neddy. He'll gallop without being kicked on.'

But the boys thought it was grand to make Neddy gallop, so they all kicked and slapped him when they rode him. The donkey-boy didn't like it, but he didn't say a word.

It wasn't much good Nora saying anything either, for the boys only laughed at her and teased her. So she tried to make up for their unkindness by bringing Neddy a few titbits. She brought him a fine carrot, which he ate up in delight. She took him an apple, and he liked that even better.

He nuzzled his big nose into Nora's hand whenever the little girl came by. He flicked his ears and shook his tail with pleasure to see her. He was always glad when someone had given her a penny so that she could ride him.

The donkey-boy liked Nora too, and he gave her a much longer ride for a penny than he gave the others. The others only went to the pier and back, but Nora went right beyond the pier to the breakwater. It was a very long ride.

Then the boys began to get cross because Nora had longer rides than they had.

'It's not fair!' they said. 'If you go as far as the breakwater, we ought to too. It's not fair!'

'Well, you mistreat old Neddy and I take him carrots and apples, so it's no wonder he likes to give me a longer ride,' said Nora. 'Why don't you ask the donkey-boy if you can go as far as I do? He's the one who decides.'

So that afternoon Jim went to have a ride, and he said to the donkey-boy, 'I'll go to the breakwater beyond the pier.'

'That will cost you twopence then,' said the boy

firmly. But Jim hadn't got twopence.

'You let Nora go as far as that for a penny,' grumbled Jim. 'It isn't fair.'

'Well, she's good to the donkey,' said the boy. 'You're not. It serves you right.'

Now Jim didn't like to quarrel with the donkey-boy for he was much bigger than Jim was – and he didn't dare to make the donkey go as far as the break-water in case the boy made him pay another penny, which he hadn't got. So he just galloped off angrily, digging his heels into Neddy's ribs.

And because he couldn't do what he wanted to, he felt very angry with poor Nora. So he made faces at her, pinched her when no one was looking, and said horrid things about her to the others.

Nora had a bad time. John, Peter, Jim, and his sister Helen teased her all the time, and she was very unhappy. But the worst time came when they all went bathing one hot, sunny morning.

'Let's get hold of Nora and duck her under!' said

Jim, with a giggle. 'Come on – there she is out there. We can easily catch her.'

'All right!' said John. 'That will teach her to have longer rides on Neddy than we do!'

So the four of them waded out to where Nora was trying to swim. She did so badly want to learn, but it was rather difficult. Every time she took her feet off the sand to try and swim with them, she seemed to go under, and she hated that.

She suddenly saw the others wading out to her, and by the look on their faces she knew they were up to mischief. 'What are you going to do?' she cried. 'Go away!'

But they came nearer and nearer, wading up to their waists. Nora could not run away because there were horrid, muddy, sinking sands beyond her, and she didn't dare to wade out deeper because she couldn't swim.

Jim caught hold of Nora. He took a quick look round the beach to make sure that no mothers or fathers were watching. No – there was only Neddy and the donkey-boy, and they didn't matter.

Nora screamed. 'Let me go! You horrid boy, let me go!'

'Come on, Helen! Come on, John! Let's all duck Nora!' called Jim, grinning. The little girl pushed him away as hard as she could, but she couldn't push all the others too. They came round her and caught hold of her swimsuit.

'Down she goes!' cried Jim. And down she went! How she spluttered and gasped and tried to catch hold of the others! The salt water went into her mouth and tasted horrid. She was frightened.

'Help! Help!' she called, getting up for a moment – but the others pushed her over again, and she sat on the sand with the water splashing her head.

There were no parents who could hear Nora – but there was Neddy! He pricked up his big ears, and knew at once that the others were teasing his friend. He shook himself free from the donkey-boy's hold and galloped down to the sea.

He trotted into the water and brayed loudly, 'Hee-haw, hee-haw, hee-haw!' That was just to let Nora know that he was coming to help her.

Neddy went right up to the children, put his head into the water, and pulled Nora up. The little girl put her arms round him, sobbing. She climbed up on to his back, and Neddy trotted to the edge of the sea with her, and she got down safely.

'Oh, thank you, Neddy,' she said – but Neddy hadn't finished his work. Oh no, there was plenty more to do yet! Back he trotted into the sea and went up to Jim, who couldn't get away from the big donkey in time. Neddy caught the boy by the back of his swimsuit and dragged him out of the water. Holding him firmly he stepped out of the water and took the wriggling Jim to a very muddy patch of sinking sand. He dropped him in – and there was poor Jim, rolling over and over in black muddy sand, trying his hardest to get out!

It was not very difficult to get out, really – but you should have seen Jim when at last he stood up and ran to firm sand. He was covered with black mud from head to foot! Neddy hee-hawed just as if he were laughing!

Then he went to fetch John, and dropped him into the mud too. And he would have got Helen and Peter, but they ran home.

'Oh, Neddy! I didn't think you were so clever!' said Nora, squeezing the water out of her hair. 'Those boys will never tease me again – and I guess they won't tease you either!'

They didn't. Neddy had taught them such a lesson that not one of the children dared to tease Nora or to hurt Neddy again. Wouldn't I have loved to see him galloping into the sea to rescue Nora!

In the Middle
of the Night

In the Middle
of the Night

HARRY WAS excited because he was going to stay with his Uncle Peter and Aunt Mary. He loved going to them, because Uncle Peter was such fun. He could play any game under the sun! He loved football and cricket and tennis, and he could run tremendously fast. Harry often used to boast about his uncle to the other boys at school.

'My Uncle Peter has a whole cupboard full of silver cups he has won for running and tennis and other things,' he said. 'You should see them! My Aunt

Mary says it takes her two days to clean them when they have to be cleaned!'

'He'd better be careful a burglar doesn't come and steal all those cups!' laughed one of the boys. 'Gosh, that would be a fine haul for anyone.'

'Pooh! No burglar could steal them,' said Harry. 'The cupboard is tightly locked, and Uncle has a big dog.'

But all the same, a robber did come and steal those silver cups! It happened while Harry was staying with his uncle and aunt too, so it was all tremendously exciting, and very upsetting. Uncle Peter, Aunt Mary and Harry had all gone out for a walk one afternoon, and Sandy, the big dog, had gone too, so the house was left quite empty.

When they all came back – what a shock for them! Someone had opened the dining-room window, slipped inside and gone to the cupboard where the silver cups were kept. A pane of glass had been neatly cut out of the front, and every single cup had been stolen! Not one was left!

'There must have been two men,' said the policeman who was called in. 'One to keep watch, and the other to do the job. I expect they had two sacks. It's a wonder they got away without anyone seeing them!'

It was a very strange thing, but not a single person had seen two men about – not even one man had been seen!

The two men who were painting the house, who had been working outside all afternoon, said that no one had been about at all. It was most puzzling.

Uncle Peter was terribly upset to lose all his beautiful cups that he was so proud of. 'They will all be melted down into silver,' he groaned. 'And that will be the last of them!'

Harry was very sad too. He did wish he could help find the thieves. But though he prowled round and asked everyone if they had seen two men with sacks, or one man with a sack, he couldn't find out anything at all.

So, after a while, nobody did anything more about it, and the police said they were doing what they could but they doubted if the thieves would be caught now.

Harry begged his uncle to lock the doors of the house very well every night. He was so afraid that the thieves might come again and steal his new aeroplane, or even his penknife, which was a very fine one he had had for his birthday. So Uncle Peter locked up every door and window, and told Harry not to worry.

One night Harry woke with a jump. He sat up in bed. Something had awakened him – what could it be? It was the very middle of the night, and everywhere was dark. Was it a noise that had awakened him?

He listened – and then he heard a sound – but it was not the noise he expected!

It was a pitiful wail from somewhere outside, and Harry's heart sank. He knew what it was – a rabbit in a trap in the field outside the garden. He had heard that noise before, and it made him very unhappy. The sound came again and again.

'Poor little bunny,' said Harry. 'It's little soft paw is caught. Oh, how I hate those traps! The poor little thing will be in pain all night long, and so terribly frightened.'

He lay down – but the sound still went on, a dreadful wail like a baby crying in the dark. Harry couldn't bear it. He was a kind boy, fond of all animals, and he hated to know that anything was being hurt.

'I can't stand this,' said Harry. 'I'm going to get up and go out into the field. Perhaps I can find the poor little thing and rescue it.'

He pulled on his jeans and his sweater and trainers. He groped about for his torch and found it in the cupboard. He slipped downstairs and out into the garden, switching on his torch to see the way he was going.

'Gosh, I hope there aren't any robbers about tonight!' thought Harry. 'I shouldn't care to meet any! I forgot about them – oh, dear! Now I'm frightened!'

He stood in the garden in the dark, and wondered if

he should go and call Uncle Peter. No, he might be cross. The rabbit wailed again and Harry forgot his fears.

'I'm not half so afraid as that poor little creature!' he said to himself. 'I'm going on!'

Down the path he went, his torch throwing a beam of light in front of him. Slugs and worms slid everywhere, and a hedgehog hurried into the garden bed. It was strange to be out in the middle of the night.

Harry came to the gate at the bottom of the garden. It led into the field. It was locked, so he climbed over it. He stood in the field grass and listened. The rabbit cried again, and Harry went towards the sound. The animal was frightened when it saw the beam of light, and lay still. Harry had to hunt for a long time before he came across the trap, and saw the rabbit there, caught by its front paw.

Harry knew how to spring the trap. He had freed animals before, and it was only a matter of a moment or two before he had set the rabbit free. He looked at the frightened animal, and whistled in surprise.

It was a pure black rabbit! Harry had expected to see the usual sandy-coloured wild rabbit – but here was a lovely creature.

'You must be a tame rabbit, escaped and gone wild again,' said Harry. 'I've a good mind to take you home with me and bathe that paw of yours. Then I might be able to find your owner and take you back. You will be safer in a nice hutch than running about the field.'

The rabbit was very tame. It stayed by Harry and let him stroke it. He lifted it up and walked back over the field with the rabbit. It was awkward climbing over the gate, but he managed it. He got back home and took the rabbit into the bathroom.

He gently bathed the hurt paw. Then he bound it up. The rabbit let him do everything without a murmur, and seemed delighted to have a friend like Harry.

'Now I wonder what I should do with you?' said the little boy. 'I know! I can put you in the box downstairs in the kitchen, the one Puss-Cat had for her kittens.'

So the rabbit slept there for the night, with a board over the top of the box so that he could not jump out and use his hurt paw.

Uncle Peter and Aunt Mary were most astonished when they heard about the rabbit and how Harry had gone to get him in the middle of the night.

'You deserve a silver cup for that!' said Uncle Peter. 'Weren't you afraid, Harry?'

'Yes, I was rather,' said Harry, blushing red. 'But I thought the rabbit must be more afraid than I was!'

Uncle Peter made a nice hutch for the rabbit, and he went to live there while his paw was getting better. Aunt Mary asked everyone she knew if they had lost a fine black rabbit, but nobody had.

'Perhaps I will be able to keep him for my own,' said Harry. 'He is such a dear, and so gentle and tame. He doesn't even run away when I put him on the lawn, Auntie.'

'Well, let him loose sometimes, if you are there to

watch him,' said Uncle Peter. 'But don't let him eat my lettuces, will you?'

Soon the black rabbit was so tame that Harry let him out every day in the garden. His paw was healed, and he was very happy. Harry played with him each day and hoped that he wouldn't hear of anyone who had lost the rabbit. He did so want to keep him for his own.

And then one morning the rabbit disappeared! Harry had gone indoors to get a book, and had left him eating the grass on the lawn – and when he came back there was no rabbit to be seen!

Harry called him, 'Bunny, Bunny, Bunny!'

But no rabbit came. Then the little boy began to look for him – and he soon found him! He had gone down to the bottom of the garden and was busy digging a burrow under the hedge there! Harry watched him. He saw how he scraped out the earth with his front paws and shot it out behind him with his back ones. When he thought the rabbit had done enough digging he picked him up and carried him back to the hutch.

Then he went to look at the tunnel the rabbit had made. He bent down and put his arm into it to see how far the rabbit had gone – and he felt something down there!

Harry took hold of it and pulled. It felt like a bit of sacking – and as he pulled, the boy heard a clinking sound. And at once a thought rushed into his head.

'I believe there's a sack buried here – with Uncle's cups in it!' he thought. 'Oh, I wonder if it is!'

He pulled and tugged, and sure enough he was right. A big sack was buried there – and Peter saw at once that it was full of the stolen silver cups. The little boy stood and thought for a moment, and then he fetched a spade. Instead of digging up the sack, he put it back and filled the hole neatly to make it all seem as if no one had been there at all. Then he hurried in to tell Uncle Peter.

His uncle and aunt were most astonished.

'And, Uncle Peter!' said Harry, in excitement. 'I've covered up the hole – and I thought if you hid in the shed nearby at night, you could see who comes to get the sack – and then you will know who the thief is!'

'I've a very good idea who the thief is now,' said Uncle Peter sternly. 'I think it's the painters. But it's a good idea of yours, Harry, to hide in the shed and catch the thieves red-handed. I'll ring up the police and tell them. I shouldn't be surprised if they fetch the sack tonight, because they are finishing the job tomorrow – and no doubt mean to take the cups with them!'

The police were most interested in Uncle Peter's news – and two policemen were sent down that night to hide in the shed with Uncle Peter. Harry begged to be allowed to hide too.

'Oh, please do let me!' he cried. 'It was my discovery. Do let me share in the excitement.'

'Very well,' said Uncle Peter. 'You may. But you're to keep inside the shed all the time – you're not to come out at all, even when we go out and catch the thief.'

So Harry promised, and that night he and Uncle Peter and the policemen all crept down silently to the shed. They slipped inside and sat down on some sacks to wait. There was a moon that night so it would be easy to spy the thief if he did come. The hedge was well lit by the moon, and Harry knew exactly where the sack was hidden.

In the middle of the night there came the sound of soft footsteps down the garden path. Someone was coming! Harry was so excited as he and the others peered out of the small window of the shed. They had cleaned it so that they might see clearly through it.

'It's Jones, the painter!' whispered Uncle Peter to the policemen. 'Just what I thought! And listen – here's someone else!'

Another figure came quietly up and spoke in a low voice. It was the man who worked with him! So there had been two thieves after all! The police had been right.

The two began to dig. Soon they came to the sack and pulled it out. The painter threw it over his shoulder and the cups made a jangling sound.

'Now!' said one of the policemen. The door of the shed was flung open and out rushed Uncle Peter and the policemen. Harry had to stay behind as he had promised, but he did wish he could go and help too. But there was no need for his help. Jones, the painter, dropped the sack in dismay, and at the same moment one policeman clicked the handcuffs round his wrists.

His accomplice was caught by the other policeman. 'He made me help him!' said the man.

'You can tell me all about that later,' said the policeman sternly. Then the two were marched off to the police car, and Harry was told to go to bed.

All Uncle Peter's cups were put back in the cupboard, after Aunt Mary and Harry had spent two whole days in cleaning them. They were very stained and dirty from their stay in the damp sack. Uncle Peter was delighted to see them back, and he stood a long time looking at them shining brightly in their glass-fronted cupboard. Then he turned to Harry.

'Well, Harry,' he said, 'it's all because of you that I got back these cups of mine! If you hadn't been brave that night and gone to get that poor rabbit – and if he hadn't dug in the garden and found that sack – I'd have lost my cups for good! I shall give you another black rabbit to match yours, Harry, and a new hutch. You can take them home when you go, and I know they will be happy with you!'

Wasn't that nice of Uncle Peter? Harry was delighted! He has a fine new hutch now, and two fat and glossy black rabbits – and seven small baby rabbits besides! Isn't he lucky?

But he deserves his luck, because he was kind and brave, the sort of boy that anyone would be pleased to have for a friend!

A Bit of Blue Sky

A Bit of Blue Sky

HARRY AND Joan badly wanted to go out in the garden to play, because Harry had a Red Indian hat of bright feathers, and he and Joan wanted to take turns at wearing it. It would be such fun to play Red Indians!

They went to the nursery window and looked out. The sky was full of clouds – big grey clouds that slid along in the wind.

Old Nannie Wimple was sitting in the nursery, knitting. She had been Daddy's Nannie when he was little, and she was very old. She had come to look after the children whilst Mummy was away, and dear me, the stories she knew, and the things she could tell

Harry and Joan! It was marvellous!

'Nannie Wimple, do you think we shall be able to go out after dinner?' asked Harry. 'Or is it going to rain?'

Nannie didn't look up from her knitting. Her needles went click-clack all the time. 'Is there enough blue sky to make a sailor a pair of trousers?' she said.

Harry and Joan stared at Nannie Wimple in surprise. What a funny thing to say!

'Why do you say that, Nannie?' asked Joan.

'Well, haven't you heard the saying that the day will be fine if you can see enough blue in the sky to make a sailor a pair of trousers?' asked Nannie Wimple.

'I think I did hear Mummy say that one day,' said Harry. 'Will it really be fine if we see enough blue sky to do that, Nannie?'

'It's quite likely to be,' said Nannie.

The two children looked up into the sky. At first they could see nothing but clouds. Then two clouds came a little apart, and the blue sky shone through, so bright that it was like a patch of forget-me-nots.

'Look!' said Joan. 'There's some blue! But, Nannie, I don't know if it's big enough to make a sailor a pair of trousers! I really don't know how much would be needed!'

'Dear, dear, these children!' said Nannie, sticking her two needles into the knitting wool and getting up to come to the window. 'I suppose I'll have to find out for you.'

'But, Nannie, however can you find out?' asked Harry in surprise.

'My great-grandmother taught me a little magic,' said Nannie. The two children suddenly felt excited. Magic! Oooh! Whatever was Nannie going to do?

'I'll get that bit of blue sky down for you, and we'll measure it up and see if there's enough for a sailor,' said Nannie. The children stared at her in surprise.

'How can you do that?' said Joan.

Nannie took a pair of big scissors, put her arm out

as far as she could, and pretended to cut the shape of the blue bit of sky. All the time she muttered some very strange-sounding words. The children knew they were magic words, and they listened in delight.

Nannie stopped muttering. She slipped her scissors into her apron pocket and pointed to the sky.

'Watch!' she said. 'That bit of blue will fall down.'

And do you know, it did! It shook itself away from the sky and began to fall to earth, getting bigger and bigger as it came! It was most extraordinary to see it tumbling down like a big blue cloth, the colour of forget-me-nots.

It fell down and down, flapping in the wind. It came into the garden! It flapped on the grass, and the children squealed for joy.

'Look! It's on the lawn! Let's go and get it!'

They rushed out to get it. They picked it up. Nannie folded it neatly, and they went indoors with the bit of blue sky.

'It's as soft as velvet and as smooth as silk,' said

Joan, feeling it. 'Isn't it lovely? Do you think there's enough to make a sailor a pair of trousers, Nannie?'

'I'm not sure,' said Nannie. 'There doesn't look *quite* enough to me!' She unrolled the bit of sky, and laid it out flat on the floor.

'That bit's enough for one leg, if it's folded over,' she said. 'And that bit, folded the other way, would be almost enough for the other leg. And there's a bit for the top of the trousers too. Dear me, I'm not sure if there's enough!'

'Oh, Nannie, does that mean it won't be fine this afternoon?' said Joan sadly.

'I'm afraid so,' said Nannie. 'There *must* be enough to make a whole pair of trousers, you know.'

'Nannie, there's enough for trousers for a *small* sailor,' said Harry eagerly. 'Don't you think so? I once saw quite a small sailor, and I'm sure this bit of sky would be big enough for *him*.'

'Well – perhaps there *is* enough for a small sailor!' said Nannie, thinking hard. 'Yes, I believe there would be. That's all right then – the weather will be fine this afternoon. Now, we must send this bit of sky back again.'

Nannie took the blue sky to the window. She opened the window and shot the sky out into the wind. The wind took hold of it and blew it away. Up, up, up it went until it reached the clouds. It squeezed itself between them, and there it shone, a nice little bit of blue sky! It was most extraordinary.

The dinner-bell rang. 'Good gracious, dinner already!' said Nannie. 'Go and wash your hands and brush your hair, both of you!'

Off they went, excited and happy. What a lovely bit of magic they had seen that morning! They ate their dinner quickly, wondering and wondering if what Nannie said was true – that the weather really would clear up and be fine.

And do you know, after their rest, which they always had until quarter-past two, the clouds were almost gone! The little bit of blue sky had got bigger and bigger and BIGGER – and now there were hardly any clouds, but blue sky everywhere!

'It's true then, it's true!' cried Joan in delight. 'Look at the lovely blue sky and warm sun! We can go out and play Red Indians all the afternoon!'

So out they went and had a lovely time. They *were* so pleased, and they told all their friends about it.

'*We'll* watch the sky next time we want fine weather too!' said their friends. 'It's a splendid thing to know that if there's enough blue sky to make a sailor a pair of trousers, then the weather will be fine!'

Did you know that? Do watch and see, will you, because you'll be so pleased if you find it is really true.

The Smugglers' Caves

The Smugglers' Caves

BILL AND David were staying at their grandmother's, down by the sea.

They were very excited because Grandpa had been telling them about the old smugglers' caves round by the big cliff.

'Oh, Grandpa! Could we explore them, do you think? Should we find anything there – you know, left by the old smugglers?' asked Bill.

Grandpa laughed. 'No! You'll find nothing but sand and shells and seaweed,' he said. 'There have been plenty of people in and out of those caves year after year. If there was anything to be found, it would have been found by now!'

'Still, it would be fun to explore them,' said David. 'We could pretend we were smugglers. Come on, Bill – we'll go this morning!'

Off they went, running down the road to the big, sandy beach, and then round the sand to where the big cliffs stuck out, steep and rocky. In these were the caves.

'Oh, look – there's a whole lot of Boy Scouts on the beach,' said Bill. 'Gosh I wish I was old enough to be a Scout. They have such fun. I bet they're going to camp somewhere here for a week or two, and bathe, and picnic, and hike all day long! Do you think they'd let us be with them sometimes?' But when the two small boys came near the company of Scouts they didn't get much of a welcome.

'You clear off, you kids,' said one of the big boys. 'This is our part of the beach, see? Don't you make yourselves nuisances here.'

The small boys went off, disappointed. 'They could

just have let us *watch* their games,' said Bill. 'We wouldn't have been a nuisance. We could even have run after their balls for them, if they went too far.'

'Oh, never mind – let's go and look for the caves,' said David. 'I'd rather explore them than watch boys who think we're too small to be anything but nuisances.'

'Here's a cave,' said Bill, and he went up to where a dark hole yawned at the foot of the cliff. 'It's a big one. Let's go in.'

They went into it. The floor was of soft sand, and seaweed hung down the sides of the walls. The sea went in and out at high tide and filled the little pools at the sides of the cave.

'It's a nice cave, but not very exciting,' said Bill. 'I don't feel as if smugglers ever came in here, do you, David? Anyway, it doesn't lead anywhere. I mean, there are no inner caves or tunnels leading into the cliff.'

'Let's find another cave,' said David. So off they

went to the next one. But that was very small, and they could hardly stand upright in it. They went out again into the sunshine.

Then they noticed a stretch of rugged rocks leading up to another cave in the cliff – a cave that really did look exciting. It had quite a small entrance. The boys climbed up the rocks to it and peered inside.

'It's nice and dark,' said Bill. 'Got your torch, David? We'll need it here.'

David switched on his torch. The boys made their way inside the cave. It was really more like a big tunnel, and it led to an inner cave. David shone his torch round. Then he gave a sudden shout.

'Bill! What's that over there? Look!'

Bill looked over to the corner into which David's torch shone. Well hidden, there were what looked like sacks and boxes. Gracious! Had they suddenly hit on some old smugglers' stores after all?

'Make sure those Boy Scouts aren't anywhere about,' said David. 'We don't want them to interfere in this. This is *our* discovery, see?'

Bill went to the outer entrance of the tunnel-like cave. He peered out. No, there were no boys about. But wait a bit – wasn't the sea a good bit nearer now?

He called to David. 'Hey! I think the tide's coming in pretty fast. Will it reach these caves, do you think? We don't want to be caught.'

'Yes. I think it *will* reach them – and then we shall be stuck here for hours,' said David. 'Blow! Just as we have found treasure, too! I don't like going off and leaving it here, with all those Scouts about. They're pretty certain to come nosing round these caves, and then they'll find it, too.'

'Well, we can't possibly take all these sacks and things down the beach with us,' said Bill. 'Won't it be all right to leave them here, David?'

'No. If *we* can find them, somebody else easily can!' said David. 'I'm surprised nobody has spotted them before. I know what we'll do, Bill.'

'What?' said Bill.

'We'll drag them to that place halfway up the cave wall,' said David, pointing. 'Do you see, there's a kind of big hole there? It may have been a proper hidy-hole once for smuggled things. I think we could drag everything up there and hide it well. We could drape some seaweed over the hole.'

It was difficult to drag everything up to the hole. The boys did not stop to open the sacks or boxes, for they were so afraid of being cut off by the tide. They managed to drag them into the hole at last, and then they hastily arranged big fronds of seaweed over the 'treasure' to hide it. When they had finished they were sure no one could possibly see it.

They slid down to the cave floor. They went cautiously to the outer entrance and peered out. They would just have time to run round the edge of the cliff before the sea was swirling all round it!

'There are the Scouts, look – in the next cave but one!' said Bill. 'I wonder what they want. They're yelling to each other rather crossly. Somebody's done something silly, I should think.'

'Well come on – let's go before they yell at *us!*' said David. The two small boys ran round the foot of the cliff, wading through a shallow stretch of water in one place. They were only just in time! The tide would soon be right up the cliff – and into some of those caves.

'The Scouts will get caught if they don't look out,' said Bill.

'Oh, they're big enough to swim if they get caught by the tide,' said David. 'Or they might even dare to climb up the cliffs!'

They went home to dinner. They told Grandpa about their exciting find, but he only laughed.

'Go on with you!' he said. 'Telling me you've found smugglers' treasure in those caves! Why, I've been in and out of them thousands of times when I was a boy. You don't suppose you could find what I didn't do you?'

'Well, but, Grandpa,' said Bill, 'we really and truly

did find treasure. At least – we didn't open the sacks because we didn't have time – but what else could be in them but old forgotten treasure?' Grandpa just laughed again. It was most disappointing of him. The boys decided not to say any more. It spoilt things if grown-ups laughed at them.

After dinner they slipped out again, hoping that the tide would soon go down and that they could once more go to the cave – and, this time, undo the 'treasure' and see what they had got!

They waded round the foot of the cliffs and came to the stretch of rocks that led up to their cave. They were soon hauling the treasure out of its hidey-hole to the floor below. 'It's a jolly good thing we put it up where we did or it would have got soaking wet,' said Bill. 'The sea came right into the cave!'

They began to open the sacks – but what a surprise they got! There was no 'treasure'! One sack was full of cups and plates and knives and forks! Another one had tins of food in it, and big loaves of bread, and about three dozen buns! One of the boxes had cricket stumps and balls in! What a very extraordinary thing!

'This isn't smugglers' treasure!' said Bill in dismay. 'But what is it? And why is it here? Who does it belong to?'

'I say – do you think it belongs to the scouts?' said David in rather a small voice. 'It's rather the sort of things they'd bring away to camp with them. I don't think we'd better undo any more.'

The boys stared at one another in dismay and fright. Had they meddled with the Scouts' belongings? How *could* they have thought they had found smugglers' treasure when they knew the sea swept in and out of that cave! How silly of them. No wonder Grandpa had laughed.

They were disappointed and miserable. 'We simply shan't dare to say a word about this to the Scouts,' said Bill, his voice trembling. 'They'd skin us alive!'

'Let's go before they discover us here with their things,' said David. So they crept out of the cave and made their way along the foot of the cliffs again. And they bumped straight into a meeting of the Scouts!

'I tell you I *did* put the things into one of the caves!' a red-faced Scout was saying. 'I did! Even if the sea had gone in, surely it wouldn't have swept *everything* out!'

'Well, not a single thing is there,' said the Scout-leader. 'And here we are, come to camp, with our food, crockery, knives and forks, everything gone! We were idiots to dump our things down like that. We should have set up camp and unpacked straight away instead of fooling about.'

'I suppose there's nothing for it but to go back home,' said another Scout, looking very blue.

Bill and David couldn't help hearing all this. They felt dreadful. It was their fault that the Scouts hadn't been able to find their things – it would be their fault if they had to give up camping and go back home.

Bill pulled David. He was scared and wanted to get

back home. But David was made of stronger stuff, and besides, he was older. He suddenly walked straight up to the Scout-leader, his face scarlet, and spoke to him.

'I'm awfully sorry – but we stuck your goods into a hidy-hole halfway up a cave-wall,' he said. 'A good thing we did, too, or they would have been soaked by the sea. You will find them in the cave quite safe.'

'You wretched little nuisances!' cried a Scout. 'You want a good telling off!'

'No, he doesn't,' said the leader. 'It was a jolly good thing he found our sacks and boxes and put them out of reach of the sea – and it can't have been an easy thing to walk up to us and confess it all, not knowing what we'd do to him. He's a good youngster, and I won't have him yelled at.'

There was a bit of grumbling, but nobody else shouted at Bill and David. 'You come along and show me which cave the things are in,' said the leader to David.

'We seem to have forgotten even which cave we used!' Bill and David took the Scouts to the cave. They were pleased when they saw all their goods. 'Now we can camp all right,' said a tall Scout. 'Thank goodness these kids had the sense to drag everything out of reach of the water.'

'We thought it was smugglers' treasure,' explained Bill, with a red face. But the Scouts didn't laugh. The leader clapped him on the back.

'You'll make a good Scout one day,' he said. 'You ought to join the Cubs, you know, you and your brother. Would you like to watch us camping? You can come to breakfast tomorrow with us if you like.'

Well, what do you think of that? The two boys beamed all over their faces.

'Oh, thanks a lot!' said David. 'We promise not to make ourselves nuisances.'

They didn't. They made themselves so useful that the Scout-leader said he really didn't know what they would do without them. And one night he even let them sleep in a tent with some of the others.

And now, as you can guess, Bill and David are both good Cubs. Are *you* a Cub or a Brownie? I'm sure you will be if you get the chance.

Mr Gobo's
Green Grass

Mr Gobo's Green Grass

THERE WAS once a funny little man called Mr Gobo. He lived in Twisty Cottage, and he had a nice little garden.

How he loved his green grass lawn! He wouldn't let a single daisy grow there. He pulled up every bit of clover. He even drove away the worms, and poured boiling water on any little brown ant he saw hurrying over the lawn.

'The Prince of Ho-Ho is coming to see me this summer,' he told everyone. 'And I am going to give him tea on my lawn. There mustn't be a single weed there, or a single worm or insect. No, not one!'

He set his little servant to work each day on the lawn. The servant was small and thin, and her name was Tiny. She had to pull the heavy roller over the grass two hundred times each day to make it smooth and even. She had to cut the grass with the lawn-mower twice a week. She had to sweep away any worm-casts that dared to show themselves in the morning.

Tiny was very tired of Gobo's beautiful green grass. She leaned over the fence and talked to the maid next door about it.

'I like the field grass,' she said. 'It has tiny flowers growing in it. It has ants and spiders and bright little beetles hurrying through it on their busy ways. I don't like Mr Gobo's lawn. It breaks my back when I have to roll it each day. If only he would do it himself!'

But Mr Gobo wouldn't do any of the hard work himself. No – Tiny must do that. He would pour hot water on a hurrying ant, or stamp on a poor worm, or pull up a small daisy – but Tiny must roll and cut and sweep.

The lawn was really beautiful. It looked like a piece of green velvet. Gobo grew more and more proud of it.

'I can't imagine what the Prince of Ho-Ho will think when he sits on it to have his tea,' he boasted. 'I am sure he has no grass as beautiful as mine. Well, he may have his palace, his hundred rooms, his golden plates – but I have a better lawn than he has!'

'But what's the use of your lawn?' asked Jinks, his next-door neighbour. 'You never play games on it. You never let your dog have a run round it. You even chase your soft-footed cat off it!'

'I should think so!' said Gobo. 'And let me tell you this, Jinks – *your* cat was stamping about on my beautiful lawn yesterday! If you don't stop her doing that, I'll shoot peas at her from my pea-shooter.'

'Don't you dare to do anything of the sort,' cried Jinks fiercely. 'I love my cat, and I won't have her hurt!'

As the day drew nearer for the Prince of Ho-Ho to come and visit him, Gobo grew more and more careful of his lawn. He shooed the birds off it. He killed every worm he found. Not an insect dared to fly over it.

Once his dog forgot, and ran lightly over the smooth green grass. Gobo was so angry that he whipped his dog till the poor dog cried.

He shot at Jinks' cat with his pea-shooter the next time it dared to walk on his lawn, and the cat bounded off in fright.

Tiny had to work with the roller and the broom till she was tired out. Up and down the lawn she went, up and down in her rubber-soled shoes, till she never wanted to see a roller, a mower, or a broom again.

The day before the prince's visit came, Gobo stood in his garden and looked proudly at his lawn. It was perfect. He was simply delighted with it. How envious the Prince of Ho-Ho would be! And how proud Gobo would feel when the prince admired his lawn!

Suddenly, as he stood there, two cars came by his gate. A dog ran across the road in front of them; they both swerved to the middle of the road to save the dog

– and CRASH! They bumped into one another!

'Oh dear, oh dear!' cried a voice from one car. 'This is such a shock! I think I shall faint!'

It was little Mother Tickles, who drove her car very carefully, because she was so afraid of accidents – and now she had had one! Her cheek was cut by the flying glass of her broken windscreen. She looked very pale indeed.

Mr Curly was in the other car. He jumped out at once and hurried to Mother Tickles in dismay. 'Now, now! Don't faint or do anything silly!' he said. 'You are not really hurt. Come along into this garden here, and I'll get some water to bathe your cheek.'

He hurried Mother Tickles into Gobo's garden gate, and made her sit down on the lawn. He shouted to Gobo, 'Bring some water! There's been an accident!'

'Please get off my grass,' said Gobo, horrified to see anyone on his precious lawn. 'Get on to the path.'

'Don't be silly,' said Mr Curly crossly. 'The grass is soft to sit on. We shan't hurt it. Get some warm water.'

Gobo was very angry. He ran up to Mother Tickles, pulled her off the grass, and sat her down hard on the dusty path. 'How dare you use my grass!' he shouted.

Jinks next door saw and heard all this. He was shocked. He called to Mr Curly, 'Bring Mother Tickles into my garden. *I'll* fetch some water and a towel.'

So poor Mother Tickles was taken into Jinks' garden and he bathed her cut cheek and looked after her. Gobo glared at them over the fence, and then went to see if his beautiful lawn had been hurt.

'You know, Mr Gobo wants a good lesson,' said Mr Curly, looking at the grass next door. 'Spending all his time making quite a useless lawn just to make the prince envious! Can't even let poor Mother Tickles sit down on it! The wretch!'

'Yes,' said Jinks slowly, looking at the grass next door. 'He *does* need a lesson. You're right! And he'll get it too, before the Prince of Ho-Ho comes! Yes, he'll get it all right!'

When Mother Tickles and Mr Curly had gone, Jinks put on his hat and went to Tibby Lickle, who was a funny old woman living alone on the hill. She knew every creature of the woods and fields, and could talk to them as easily as she could talk to Jinks.

'Tibby Lickle,' said Jinks, 'I want something done.'

'And what's that?' asked old Tibby Lickle, her bright green eyes twinkling up at Jinks. 'I'll do anything for *you*, Jinks. You're a good kind fellow. That I know!'

'Well, Tibble Lickle, what I'm asking you to do will not seem kind,' said Jinks, 'but it needs to be done. Now, I want you to go the moles, who live under the ground, and ask them to tunnel up and down beneath Mister Gobo's lawn tonight. Will you do that?'

'Indeed I will,' said old Tibby Lickle, and she went straight off to give the message.

And that night six velvety moles tunnelled underground till they came to Gobo's beautiful lawn. And then, all night long they tunnelled below his grass, making passages underneath it, up and down, up and down. Here and there they threw up hillocks of fine earth on the grass. How those moles worked – and then they slipped away silently along their underground passages.

And when Gobo awoke next morning and looked out of the window, *what* a shock he got! His lawn was completely spoilt! It was bumpy and uneven, where the moles had tunnelled beneath it. It was covered with hillocks of earth. It wasn't a lawn at all!

'Oh! Oh! Look at that!' he wept. 'Tiny, where are you? Oh, look at that!'

Tiny stood and looked at the lawn. 'Ah, master,' she said, 'you wouldn't let an old woman sit on your precious lawn yesterday – and now it is spoilt! It serves you right! Whatever will the prince say?'

The prince came – and how he did turn up his nose at poor Gobo's spoilt lawn!

'Dear me!' he said. 'You must take a few lessons from one of my gardeners, Gobo! This is dreadful!

How you have let your lawn go to pieces!'

'I don't need any lessons,' said Gobo, his face very red. 'I've had one big lesson – and that's quite enough for me! In future my lawn isn't going to be beautiful – it's going to be useful!'

And so it is. The dog plays on it, the cat washes herself there, the birds fly down to it, and the worms have a fine time. What could you want better than that?

Smokey and the
Seagull

Smokey and the Seagull

'I WISH my mistress wouldn't put my dinner out of doors,' said Smokey the cat to his friend Sooty. Smokey was on the wall with him, and their long tails hung down, twitching just a little.

'Why? What does it matter if she does?' said Sooty. 'It tastes just the same, indoors or out!'

'I know. But there's a big seagull that comes in from the beach,' said Smokey, 'and he sits on our roof and watches for my mistress to come out with my dinner – it's always a nice bit of fish, you know, and that seagull loves fish! And as soon as he sees my mistress coming out with my dish, down he flies to it and gobbles up my dinner!'

'Well, I wonder you allow that!' said Sooty, swinging his black tail angrily as he thought of the greedy seagull. 'I have my dinner indoors, thank goodness!'

'My mistress won't let me have it there,' said Smokey, mournfully. 'She says I make too much mess. So what am I to do?'

'Pounce on the seagull, of course,' said Sooty. 'That's easy.'

'Sooty – have you ever seen a seagull close to?' asked Smokey. 'Do you know how big it is?'

'No, I never go down on the beach,' said Sooty. 'I don't like walking in soft sand – it's like snow, and my paws sink right down.'

'Well – a seagull is enormous,' said Smokey. 'I wouldn't dare to pounce on it.'

'Well, just pounce on its tail, then,' said Sooty. 'And hang on for all you are worth. Pull out a few feathers if you can – then that seagull won't come again!'

'Yes, that may be quite a good idea,' said Smokey. 'It is its beak I'm scared of – it's so big and strong. I really believe it could bite off my tail!'

'Well, you get hold of the seagull's tail first!' said Sooty. 'I'll sit up here and cheer you on. Do be brave, Smokey.'

'That's all very well,' said Smokey. 'You'd think twice before you pounced on a great seagull! Still, I'll try it. I'll hide behind the dustbin and wait till the gull comes down. Then, when it has its back to me, I'll pounce!'

'What time do you have your dinner?' asked Sooty. 'I really must watch this.'

'When that big clock over there strikes one,' said Smokey. 'Mistress comes out just after that. Sooty, will you come to my help if I need it?'

'Of course. Certainly!' said Sooty. 'I'll leap right on top of the gull and bite his neck!'

'You are brave!' said Smokey, admiringly. 'All right – watch out for my mistress to come at dinner-time.'

He jumped down from the wall and ran off to the house. Just before he went indoors he looked up at the sky. There were the big seagulls, gliding to and fro on the breeze, their enormous wings spread wide. Smokey wondered which of them was the one that stole his dinner!

He smelled his fish cooking on the kitchen stove and felt hungry. Yesterday the seagull had gobbled all his dinner up, and poor Smokey had only been able to lick out the dish. How he hoped he would be able to eat it all himself today!

'Are you hungry, little cat?' asked his mistress. 'Well, you shall have your fish as soon as it is cool. Don't keep walking round my legs like that – it won't make your dinner come any quicker!'

When the big clock struck one, Sooty jumped up on the wall to see if Smokey really did mean to pounce on the sea-gull. He saw his friend come running out of the house and then he hid behind the dustbin. Only the tip of his whiskers could be seen.

Overhead a big gull spread its white wings and waited for Smokey's dinner to arrive!

Sooty gazed up at it and felt quite scared when he saw how big it was.

Goodness – would Smokey be brave enough to pounce on that enormous bird?

Smokey saw the gull too and hissed and spat. That greedy gull! Well, Smokey meant to pounce on him if he possibly could. He saw Sooty up on the wall, watching. He would show him how brave he was!

Smokey's mistress came out with his dish of fish. How good it smelled!

'Smokey, Smokey!' she called. 'Dinner! Where are you!'

Smokey stayed behind the dustbin waiting. His mistress went indoors.

As soon as she had disappeared, the big seagull glided down on outspread wings. It landed on the lawn and closed its wings, then walked quickly over to the dish, turning its back on Smokey. It was just about to peck up a large mouthful of fish when Smokey shot out from his hiding place, and pounced on the seagull's tail. He gripped it with claws and teeth, pulling with all his might.

The gull was very frightened. It gave a loud cry, spread its wings and rose up into the air – and what a sight to see – it took poor Smokey with it!

You see, Smokey hadn't had time to let go of the tail, and there he was, up in the air with the gull, hanging on to the tail-feathers for dear life!

Sooty watched with amazement. Now what would happen? Poor Smokey! Would he be taken right out to sea, and shaken off into the big waves?

The seagull was just as frightened as Smokey. It took a quick look round and saw that the heavy weight on its tail was a little black cat! It didn't know what to do! It couldn't peck him off in mid-air.

And then something most peculiar happened. The tail-feathers could no longer bear the weight of the cat – and they broke off! So, of course, poor Smokey fell from the seagull, the tail-feathers still in his mouth and claws, and found himself falling, falling through the air. He was very frightened and Sooty, on the wall, miaowed in horror.

But, like all cats, Smokey landed on his feet. He found himself on the lawn, very shaken and surprised, but unhurt. He sat down to get his breath, his mouth full of white tail-feathers! Sooty called out to him.

'Smokey! Are you hurt? My – aren't you brave!'

Smokey spat out the tail-feathers, and looked proudly at Sooty. 'Well – I won, didn't I? I've saved my dinner and pulled out the seagull's tail – though I didn't really mean to. I *was* surprised when he flew up into the air with me.'

'Good old Smokey!' said Sooty. 'I really must tell all the other cats about this. Come with me, Smokey. You'll be a hero!'

'No, I want my dinner before I'm a hero,' said Smokey and ran to his dish. He gobbled up all the fish, and didn't even bother to keep a look-out for the seagull – no – he had defeated him for always! That gull would never dare come back.

Smokey was right. The big seagull kept well away from the gardens after that. Sooty and Smokey sat on the wall, looking up into the sky day after day – and how they miaowed when they saw the gull without a tail!

'There he is! Miaow-miaow! How strange he looks. We'll always know him now.'

But they won't. The seagull's tail-feathers are already growing again, and soon he will look just like the others. What a shock he had that day when Smokey pounced on his tail – and what a hero Smokey is now!

Adventures Under the Sea

Adventures Under the Sea

DICK WAS fast asleep one night when there came
flying in at his bedroom window a fairy dressed in
blue and green.

'Wake up, wake up!' cried the fairy.

Dick woke with a jump, and sat up.

'What do you want?' he asked.

'Are you the little boy who picked up a jellyfish
that was lying in the sun and kindly put it into a pool
again?' asked the fairy.

'Yes, I did, this morning,' answered Dick.

'Well, when it got back into its home, it found the
King of the Sea and asked if you might, for a treat,

be taken under the sea to the sea fairies' home,' said the fairy.

'Oh, I'd *love* to come!' cried Dick.

'Come down to the seashore quickly, then, just as you are,' said the fairy. 'I'll meet you there.'

Dick slipped downstairs, and was away on the beach ever so quickly. Across the water stretched a shimmering path of moonlight.

'Hold my hand,' said the sea fairy, 'and we'll run along the moon-path.'

Dick didn't think it would hold him, but it did. And off the two went, running along the bright moon-path over the waves.

At last they stopped. 'Now,' said the fairy, 'shut your eyes while I say some magic words to make you able to go down to my home.'

Dick shut his eyes, and the fairy sang some strange-sounding words. Dick felt himself sinking down and down and down.

'Oh,' he cried, when he opened his eyes, 'what a

lovely place!'

He was standing in a great blue-green hall, decorated with long streamers of waving seaweed. At one end sat Neptune, the King of the Sea, with a crown of beautiful shells.

'Welcome!' he said. 'It isn't often I have a visitor from above the sea. Would you like to see some of the wonderful things here?'

'Oh, yes please,' said Dick.

Neptune turned to the blue and green fairy. 'Pearl,' he said, 'show Dick round our sea home.'

'Come along, Dick,' said Pearl.

'Dear me!' said Dick, staring at her, 'whatever have you done with your legs, Pearl?'

'Oh, I only use legs for the land,' laughed Pearl. 'I put a tail on down here. Isn't it a nice one?' and off she swam, with Dick following.

They came to a dark, quiet cave, in which sat a solemn little merman with a long yellow tail. He had a silvery net, and was gazing up through the water.

'What's he doing?' asked Dick.

'Look up,' said Pearl. 'Can you see those shining things right up there on the top of the water?'

'Yes,' said Dick. 'They're stars reflected in the sea, aren't they?'

'Yes! Watch,' said Pearl.

The merman suddenly flung his net up into the water. It rose up and up. When he pulled it down again Dick saw it was full of faint shining stars.

'He caught the stars you saw reflected on the top of the water,' said Pearl.

The merman picked out the smallest, and threaded them on a fine string.

'They're for the baby sea fairies to play with,' he said. 'The rest I throw away; they're too big.'

He threw a lot down on the ground. To Dick's surprise they turned pink and slowly moved away.

'Goodness me,' he cried, 'they've turned into starfish!'

'Yes, they always do that,' answered Pearl. 'Now

you know why they're shaped like stars. Come along!'

She took him out into a wide, open, sandy place, with rocks all around and beautiful sea flowers. Playing about were baby sea fairies, all with tails.

'Would you like to see them play their favourite game?'

'Yes, I would,' answered Dick.

Pearl went to a big square rock and opened the top, just like a box-lid. All the baby fairies swam over to her, calling out:

'Our balloons, our balloons!'

'Oh, you're giving them jellyfish!' cried Dick in surprise.

'Yes, they're not like *your* balloons,' laughed Pearl, 'and they're made of jelly, so that they don't burst and frighten the babies.'

Dick watched the little fairies. Each held on to the streamers hanging down from the jellyfish, and away they floated, up and up, carried by their strange balloons.

'Oh,' cried a baby, tumbling down, 'mine is broken!' His jellyfish went sailing away by itself. Soon three or four more babies came tumbling down, laughing and rolling on the sand.

'There go their balloons!' cried Dick.

'Yes,' said Pearl, 'and I expect you'll find them floating about helplessly somewhere at the edge of the sea tomorrow, with their strings hanging down.'

'I often wondered what use jellyfish were,' said Dick. 'I'm so glad I know now.'

'Now we'll go and see the white horses,' said Pearl, swimming off.

'Oh, are there *really* white horses in the sea?' asked Dick. 'I thought they were just white foam on the top of waves.'

'Dear me, no!' said Pearl. 'When they gallop along under the sea, and make big waves come, it's their curly white manes you can see peeping up here and there – not just white foam!'

'Oh, there they are!' cried Dick. There in front of

him stretched a wide field of green seaweed, and munching it were great white horses with beautiful curly manes of snow-white.

'Stroke one,' said Pearl, 'they're quite tame.'

Dick stroked one, and it felt as soft as foam.

'I'm going to let one take you home,' said Pearl. 'Jump on his back.'

Dick climbed up.

'Goodbye!' called Pearl. 'I'm glad you came.'

'Goodbye!' shouted Dick, holding on to the thick mane of his horse as it galloped off.

When it got to the seashore it stood still. Dick slipped off and watched it disappear into the waves.

'*What* a lovely night I've had!' he said, as he ran back home again and cuddled down into bed.

An Exciting
Afternoon

An Exciting Afternoon

TOM WAS out on his bicycle one lovely afternoon. He was bird-watching.

He was very keen on nature, especially birds, and he knew more about them than anyone else at school. For his birthday his father had given him a wonderful present. It was a pair of binoculars.

He could see birds a long way away with them. It was such fun to sit down by a hedge, put his binoculars to his eyes, and watch a bird at the other end of the field. He could see what it did without frightening it at all.

Tom was sitting down, perfectly quiet, his

binoculars to his eyes, when somebody came along the road. Tom took no notice. He was watching a yellowhammer singing on the topmost branch of a bush a long way away.

The somebody stopped when he saw Tom's bicycle propped against the hedge. He looked round cautiously. He could not see Tom on the other side. So, in a flash, the man took the bicycle, jumped on it, and pedalled off furiously down the lane!

Tom heard the noise and jumped up. He leaned over the gate by the hedge. His bicycle was gone – and there, away down the road, was a man riding it at top speed.

'Hey! Stop! That's my bike!' yelled Tom. But the man didn't stop, of course. He had a bag over his shoulder, and he pedalled along at about thirty miles an hour!

Tom was very angry. But what could he do? He could never catch the man up. Now he would have to walk home – and home was at least eight miles away.

He had better start now, for it would take him ages.

'A lovely afternoon spoilt,' said Tom, gloomily. He stepped out down the lane, listening to another yellowhammer calling out something about bread and cheese.

Soon he came to the main road. After a while a car came along. It was a police car. In the car were two burly policemen, whose keen eyes looked Tom up and down.

'What are you doing walking out here on your own?' asked the driver.

Tom went red. 'I've had my bike stolen,' he said. 'And now I have to walk home.'

'Oh! So you've had your bicycle stolen have you?' said the second policeman. 'I suppose you're some way from home, then?'

'About eight miles,' said Tom.

'Then jump in and tell us about it,' said the policeman. 'We'll take you part of the way home, at any rate.'

So Tom got in, feeling rather grand to be in a police car. The driver started up the engine and they shot off down the road.

Tom began to tell them about how his bicycle had been stolen. The car slid swiftly along as he told his tale.

And, just as Tom finished his story, he saw something that made him sit up straight in the back of the car.

'Look! There's my bike! That must be the man who stole it, too, who's riding it now. I remember that he had a sack or something over his shoulder.'

The policeman slowed down the car. 'We'll ask him a few questions,' said the driver, grimly. 'Sure it's your bike, lad?'

'Oh, yes. I'd know it anywhere!' said Tom, in excitement. The police car shot by the man on the bicycle, came to a stop – and, just as the man reached the car, out jumped the two policemen!

The man almost fell off the bicycle with fright. One

of the policemen caught hold of the handlebars, and the man had to get off.

'Where did you get this bicycle?' asked the policeman.

'It's mine!' said the man. 'Keep your hands off it. Let me go!' He tried to jump on and ride off, but he couldn't.

'Let's see what you've got in your sack,' said the other policeman, and deftly took the sack from the man's shoulder. He opened it and gave a loud exclamation.

'Whew! Look here!'

Tom and the other policeman looked. The sack was full of silver candlesticks, gold boxes and jewel cases.

'He's the fellow who has just robbed Lady Landley!' said the driver. 'My word – we've only just got the message through and we've got the thief! You'll have to come with us, man.'

'Can I have my bicycle back?' asked Tom, eagerly.

'Oh, yes. He took it to make a quick getaway,' said

one of the policemen. 'What a good thing you got a lift from us, sonny, and saw the fellow riding your bicycle. You get back your bike, Lady Landley gets back her property – and we get a very clever thief that we've been hunting for a very long while! A good afternoon's work!'

'It's been a most exciting afternoon!' said Tom. 'And there's still time for me to go and do some bird-watching after all – but I think I really must go home and tell my mother and brother and sister what's happened. Good gracious – it's even more exciting than bird-watching!'

He rode off, and the policemen bundled the thief into the car and drove him to a police station. How surprised he was to be caught so quickly!

'How exciting!' thought Tom, as he pedalled quickly home. 'Really, you never know what's going to happen!'

Lazy Lenny

Lazy Lenny

LENNY WAS lucky. He was down by the sea for a holiday, with his three cousins, Karen, Rachel and George. They were having great fun. They all had fishing-nets, spades, pails and balls, so there was plenty for them to do.

The only thing was – Lenny was so lazy. He would only dig for a few minutes in the sand, and then stop. He would only fetch water two or three times in his pail and then he wanted to lie down in the sun. The others thought he was very tiresome.

'He leaves us to finish everything,' said Karen. 'He's lazy.'

'It would do him good to dig hard every day,' said George. 'He's too fat.'

'He just digs a few spadefuls and then leaves us to do all the hard work,' said Rachel. 'And when we have finished our castle, or our moat, he expects to be allowed to sit on the top, or paddle in the moat. It's not fair.'

'I vote we *make* him work hard today,' said Karen. 'We will dig a simply enormous castle, and we will make him help. We just won't let him say no!'

So when they were down on the beach that day Karen spoke to Lenny.

'Lenny, we're going to build the most enormous castle we have ever built before. You're to help us.'

'It's too hot to dig,' said Lenny, lazily.

'We're not going to listen to excuses like that,' said George, crossly. 'You've got to do your bit. Come on, now – get up and help.'

'I've left my spade at home,' said Lenny, lying back on the sand.

'We'll soon put that right,' said Karen, and she ran up the beach, across the road, and into the house where they were all staying. She soon came back with Lenny's spade. 'There you are, Lazy!' she said, throwing it down beside him. 'Now come and dig.'

'My spade is so bent, it's no use,' said Lenny. He really was marvellous at making excuses.

The other children looked at the spade. It was an iron one, and certainly it had got rather bent.

'Well, George has two spades. He will lend you one of his,' said Rachel, impatiently. 'George, throw it across.'

George threw his second spade across to Lenny. It hit him on the ankle.

'Oooh, oooh!' said Lenny, pretending to be hurt, and rubbing his ankle. 'Now I shan't be able to stand!'

'Don't be a baby,' said Karen. 'Get up and dig.'

'I'm not going to use that silly baby wooden spade,' said Lenny. 'It's too small for me.'

'Well, what are you going to do then?' asked Karen.

'Aren't you ever going to dig again?' You say you can't use your spade because it's bent, and you won't use George's because it's a wooden one. What are you going to do?'

'My mother gave me some money this morning to buy a new spade,' said Lenny, and he took a pound out of his pocket to show the others. 'I shall get one at that nice shop on the corner, that has hundreds of spades hanging outside.'

'Well, go and buy it now, then, and you can help us to dig,' said George. 'Go on. Get up and buy it. You are always making excuses.'

'I just want to see these aeroplanes flying over,' said Lenny, and he lay on his back to watch them. The others began their digging. Lenny watched the planes and played with his money. The planes flew right over and disappeared.

'Go on, Lenny, and buy your spade now,' said Karen. 'The planes have gone.'

'I want to watch that dog having a bathe,' said

Lenny. 'Don't bother me. I'll go in a minute.'

The dog splashed in and out of the water, barking. Then he ran to his master. The three children looked at Lenny. He knew he would have to go now. He could think of no more excuses.

So up he got and brushed the sand from his shorts. Then he felt in his pocket for the pound he had been playing with.

It wasn't there! He felt again and again, but no, the pound was gone. It must have fallen into the sand. He bent down to look for it.

'What's the matter now?' asked George.

'I've lost my pound,' said Lenny. 'Come and help me to look for it.'

'No,' said George. 'You can see we are busy. You wouldn't come and help us when we asked you to. I don't see why we should stop digging our castle to dig for your pound. You find it yourself!'

Well, poor Lenny hunted the whole of the morning for that pound, and he couldn't find it! It was most extraordinary. He took George's little wooden spade and dug up the sand all round him, working so hard that he panted like a dog. But he couldn't find anything.

'Look at Lenny! He's working far harder than we wanted him to!' laughed Karen. She couldn't help feeling a bit sorry for Lenny, because she knew how horrid it is to lose anything. But she felt that it was very good for him to have to work so hard to find it.

Dinnertime came and still the money was not found. Lenny went home in tears and told his mother. She was cross.

'I shall not give you another pound,' she said. 'Why didn't you stop at the shop on your way down to the beach and buy a new spade at once, as I told you to? I knew you would lose it if you took it down on the sand.'

'I haven't a spade to dig with,' wept Lenny. 'Mine's bent.'

'Well, I'll give you my wooden one,' said George.

'You didn't want it this morning, but now that you can't get a new one, perhaps you would like it.'

'And you can use my spade when I'm not digging if you like,' said Karen, kindly.

'And mine too,' said Rachel, slipping her hand into Lenny's. He felt comforted.

'You're kind,' he said. 'I wouldn't help you this morning, but all the same you want to help *me*. I won't be lazy again. I'll help you to dig this afternoon, and I'll dig like anything. You just see! You haven't quite finished the castle, so there's still some to be done.'

'Good boy!' said Karen. 'That's the way to talk. We'll think a lot of you if you behave like that.'

Lenny ate his dinner and thought quite a lot while he ate it. He knew he was lazy. He knew that he left most of the hard work to his cousins. Now he had lost his pound because he had been too lazy to dig, too lazy to go and get his new spade, too lazy to do anything but lie in the sand and watch the others at work.

'But now I'm going to behave properly,' he decided.

'I'll show the others what I can really do. I'm sure I dug harder in the sand, looking for my pound this morning, than they dug when they were building their castle!'

So that afternoon, when they went down on the beach, it was a very different Lenny who set to work on the castle. The others were nice to him.

'That spade of George's really is too small for you,' said Karen. 'I'll lend you mine and use the wooden one instead. I don't mind.'

'No – he can have my big spade,' said George, generously. 'Here you are Lenny.'

'I'll go and fetch water for the moat round the castle, and Lenny can use my spade,' said Rachel.

Lenny looked at her. 'But you don't like fetching water. You like digging,' he said.

'Oh, well, that doesn't matter,' said Rachel, and she picked up her pail. She pushed her spade into Lenny's hand and he began to dig.

He dug two or three times, lifting up big loads to

put on top of the high castle – and then, as he lifted up the third spadeful, something fell from the sand into the moat round the castle – something round.

'Oh – my POUND!' yelled Lenny, in the greatest surprise and delight. 'Look – my pound!'

He picked it up. The others crowded round him, just as pleased as he was. 'Now you'll be able to buy yourself a new spade after all!' said Karen. 'Oh, I *am* glad you've found it.'

'I'm going off to the shop straight away,' said Lenny, and he sped off up the beach and on to the front. He went to the shop that sold spades – but he didn't buy a spade. No – he bought a tiny red and blue boat for Karen that cost forty pence. He bought a floating fish for Rachel that cost fifteen pence. And he bought a little grey battleship for George that cost forty-five pence. That made up the pound.

He rushed back to the beach. 'George! Karen! Rachel! Look what I've got for you!'

The children looked and were thrilled. 'Oh, what

lovely little things,' said Karen. 'But didn't you buy yourself a spade then, Lenny?'

'No,' said Lenny. 'I'll use George's old one, if he'll let me. There wasn't anything wrong with it really. All that was wrong was my own laziness! These little presents for you are my way of saying I'm sorry. Come on – let's finish the castle.'

Well, wasn't that fine of Lenny! The other children thought the world of him after that, and when they told their own mother what Lenny had bought with his pound, what do you think she did? Yes – she went off and bought a new spade for Lenny – so everyone was as pleased as could be!

Pink Paint
for a Pixie

Pink Paint for a Pixie

ONCE, WHEN Linda was playing at the bottom of her garden, she heard a funny noise. She stopped and listened.

'If a bird could speak, it would speak just like that funny voice,' thought Linda, in surprise. 'It *is* somebody talking – it's a very small voice, high and clear.'

She sat perfectly still, listening, trying to hear what the voice said.

'Just my luck!' said the voice. 'Finished the tea-set all but three cups – and now I've run out of paint. Isn't that just my luck?'

Linda quietly popped her head through a gap in the hedge to see who could be talking. It didn't at all sound like a child. It wasn't a child, either.

'It's a pixie!' said Linda, in the greatest surprise. 'Well, who would have thought I'd ever see a pixie! I've looked for years and years and never seen one. But this *must* be one – and he's talking to himself. What is he doing?'

She looked closely and saw that he was painting a very small tea-set, just big enough for himself to drink from. The cups and saucers were about the size of the ones in Linda's doll's house.

Suddenly the tiny fellow heard Linda breathing and he looked up. He stared in surprise at the little girl's head peeping through the hedge.

'Hallo!' he said. 'Isn't it a nuisance – I've run out of pink paint.'

'What are you doing?' asked Linda.

'I'm painting a pretty pattern on these cups,' said the pixie, and he held one up for Linda to see.

He certainly was putting a very pretty pattern on each one. There were pink roses and green leaves all the way around. The saucers and plates had the same pattern.

Linda looked at the tiny tubes of paint beside the pixie. The tube of pink paint was squeezed quite empty.

'Can't you finish your work?' she asked.

'No,' said the pixie. 'And I promised the Princess Peronel she should have the whole set tomorrow, for her birthday party. It's really annoying.'

Linda suddenly had a splendid idea. *She* had some tubes of paint in her paint box. One might be pink. If so, she could lend it to the pixie!

'I believe I could help you,' she said. 'I've got some paints. I'll go and get the tube of pink. Wait here a minute.'

She ran indoors and found her paint box. 'Darling, surely you are not going to paint indoors this fine morning!' said her mother, when she saw Linda getting out her paint-box.

'No, Mummy – I'm lending a tube of pink paint to a pixie,' said Linda.

Her mother laughed. 'What funny things you do say, Linda!' she said. She didn't guess for a minute that Linda was speaking the truth. She thought she was just pretending.

Linda ran out again, holding in her hand a tube of crimson paint. She knew that if the pixie mixed the deep red with water, the colour would be pink. She was soon back at the hedge again.

'Here you are,' she said. 'I'm sure this will make a lovely pink.'

'You *are* a good friend!' said the pixie, gratefully. 'You can watch me paint if you like.'

Linda sat and watched him. He had a tiny china palette on which he mixed his colours. He squeezed some of the crimson out on to it, and then dipped his tiny brush into a dewdrop hanging on a grass nearby. Soon he had just the right pink for the little cups. It was fun to watch him painting roses round the cup he was holding.

'I don't know what I should have done if you hadn't helped me,' he said. 'Can I do anything for you in return?'

'I suppose you couldn't make a wish come true, could you?' asked Linda, at once. The pixie shook his head.

'No,' he said. 'I don't know powerful enough magic for that. If I did I'd have wished for a new tube of pink paint for myself. But if you really want a wish to come true why don't you find a four-leaved clover, put it under your pillow, and wish before you go to sleep?'

'There aren't any four-leaved clovers round about here,' said Linda. 'I and the other children have looked and looked, but we have never found one.'

'Well, go to where the foxgloves grow, pick up a fallen foxglove bell, slip it on your thumb and wish,' said the pixie.

'The foxgloves aren't out yet,' said Linda.

'Of course they aren't!' said the pixie. 'How silly of me. Well, try the pink-tipped daisy spell, then.'

'What's that?' asked Linda.

'You pick thirteen pink-tipped daisies,' said the pixie. 'You make them into a daisy-chain, and wear them round your neck for one hour, at four o'clock in the daytime. You wish your wish thirteen times in that hour. Then you take off the chain and put the daisies in water. You mustn't forget to do that, because if you don't give them a drink, the magic won't work.'

'That sounds a good spell,' said Linda. 'But there aren't any pink-tipped daisies round here, pixie. Look – they are quite white.'

The little girl picked two or three daisies and showed them to the pixie. He looked underneath the petals at the very tips. He shook his head.

'You're right,' he said. 'Not a pink tip to be seen. Very tiresome. Well, I must think of something else for you.'

A bell rang in the distance. Linda got up. 'That's

for my dinner,' she said. 'I must go. I'll come back again afterwards.'

'I'll think of something whilst you are gone,' said the pixie. He thought and he thought. But he could think of no other way of making a wish come true. He was only a small pixie, not very old, and he really didn't know a great deal of magic.

Then a fine idea came into his small head. Hadn't he got plenty of pink paint in that tube? Well, why shouldn't he paint all the daisies round about with pink tips?

'Good idea!' he said, and as soon as he finished his tea-set, he went to the daisies, sat underneath the little flowers, and carefully ran his brush, full of pink paint, under the tip of each petal. Soon the first daisy looked really pretty. It turned up its petals a little to show the pink underneath.

'I hope Linda comes back soon,' thought the pixie. 'Then I can tell her what I've done.'

But Linda didn't come back. Her mother had said

she must have a rest after dinner, and the little girl was on her bed, hoping that the pixie would still be in the field when she got up at three o'clock.

He wasn't. He had packed up his painted tea-set for the Princess Peronel and had gone. But there were the daisies, all pink-tipped! And there was the little tube of paint left beside them, half-empty now, with the top put neatly on.

Linda looked round for the pixie, when she crept out through the hedge into the field after her rest. He wasn't there. But there was her tube of paint – and, oh, what a surprise, it was lying by a daisy-plant, where four pink-tipped daisies grew together, their golden eyes looking straight at Linda!

'He's painted your tips pink! The underneath of your pretty white petal is crimson pink! Now I can try that magic spell!'

Linda picked thirteen daisies and made them into a chain. You know how she made it, don't you? She slit each stalk near its end with a pin, and then slipped a daisy through the slit, so that soon the thirteen were hanging in a pretty chain. She joined the chain – and looked at her watch.

'Four o'clock! Now I'll wear it – and for one hour I will wish my wish thirteen times!'

She wore the daisy-chain, and wished her wish thirteen times in the hour. Then she took off the chain and put the daisies into water to have a drink. She wished for her big soldier-brother to come back from far away – and, will you believe it, he came home the very next day. She rushed out to tell the pixie, but she has never seen him again.

Have you seen pink-tipped daisies? Go out and look for some; maybe you will find thirteen!

Shut The Gate

Shut The Gate

'HEY, YOU there! Shut the gate, can't you?' roared a voice. Pat and Biddy turned round. A big man was standing in a field by the lane, pointing with his stick at the gate they had left open behind them.

Pat ran back and shut the gate. Biddy felt scared when the big man came out of his field and walked up to her.

'Hasn't anyone ever told you to shut gates behind you?' he said, crossly. 'Haven't you got enough brains to shut them yourselves even without being told?'

'We *have* been told,' said Biddy, going red. 'I'm sorry we forgot. Does it matter very much?'

'Matter very much?' roared the farmer, his voice very loud again. 'Now, you use your common sense! What keeps those horses in the field? What keeps my sheep from wandering into the road? What stops those calves over there from running out and getting lost or knocked down?'

'The gate,' said Pat, scared. Biddy couldn't say a word. She wanted to run away.

'Yes, the gate,' said the farmer. 'What are you doing in my fields, anyway?'

'Well, we're very fond of animals,' said Pat. 'We love horses, and we like cows. Biddy loves the little calves, and we like going to watch the lambs frisking about. Does it matter going into the fields to talk to them?'

'Not if you always shut the gates behind you,' said the farmer. 'I like to see children fond of animals – but I don't like to see them letting horses and cows run the risk of getting loose in the road, and maybe knocked down by a car. You mind what you're doing!'

He walked off. Pat and Biddy went home without saying a word. They felt very guilty. Uncle Ben and Auntie Sue were always warning them about shutting gates – yes, and doors, too. If the kitchen door or any other door was left open the hens and ducks walked in.

It was lovely staying in the country with Auntie Sue. It was glorious to wake up in the morning and hear the hens clucking just outside the window, the ducks quacking on the pond nearby and the clop-clop of horses' hoofs in the yard. It was much, much better than being in a town.

Pat and Biddy loved every single bird and animal round about. They even loved the big old sow, and they adored her nine baby pigs. But perhaps most of all, they loved Bray, the donkey.

He was grey, with long ears and a tail that swished the flies away very cleverly. He had a way of coming sideways up to the children, rubbing himself against them and putting his big grey nose on to their shoulders.

'He likes us as much as we like him,' said Biddy, in delight. 'I'm going to save my lumps of sugar for him each day instead of putting them in my cocoa.'

'And I shall bring him a carrot if Uncle will let me,' said Pat. 'And I shall brush him and clean him just as if he was a horse.'

Bray gave them rides. He cantered with them and even galloped once or twice, which felt very grand and exciting. The children went to see him as often as they could, and whenever he saw them coming he trotted to the gate to meet them.

'I wish he was ours,' said Pat. 'He's not, but he does seem to belong to us two, doesn't he, Biddy?'

'Yes, he does. Shan't we miss him when we go back home!' said Biddy. 'Pat, let's ask Uncle if we can borrow his camera and take a picture of him, shall we? I'd love a photo of Bray to take home.'

Bray used to have a little donkey-cart to draw along, but now he was old and he didn't do anything except have a good time in the field, and talk to the horses when they came back from work at night.

'But he doesn't really *seem* old, does he?' said Pat to Biddy. 'He canters and brays and he's not a bit patchy in his coat, like some old animals are.'

Uncle Ben and Auntie Sue were amused at the way the children fussed over Bray.

'Yes, he's a nice old thing,' said Uncle Ben. 'But he's been a rascal in his time. There was a year when he kept getting through the hedge and wandering into people's gardens and doing a lot of damage. We really thought he did it out of mischief! He had a lot of beatings then.'

'*Beatings!*' said Biddy in horror. 'Did you ever beat dear old Bray? Oh, poor thing! But you won't ever beat him again, will you, Uncle?'

'I shouldn't think so,' said Uncle Ben, smiling. 'Dear me, Biddy, is that sugar for Bray again? No wonder he loves you so much!'

Bray and the horses lived in a field quite near to the

house. You had to go up the garden, out of the little gate at the top, up the lane a little way and then through the big five-barred gate into the field. And, at the gate waiting for them would be Bray, his long, grey nose over the top bar, his eyes looking for them down the lane.

One day they were not allowed to go and see Bray. Auntie Sue was very cross with them. 'Just look!' she scolded, standing in their bedroom. 'Clothes on the floor – the card game you were playing last night still scattered all over the place – your beds not made – every cupboard and drawer left open! I will not have such carelessness and untidiness. Now you begin straightaway and clear up. And sew that button on your jacket, Biddy. Oh, yes, you *can* sew it on all right, even if it *is* a bit stiff to get the needle through the thick material. And you take your dirty, muddy boots down to the yard and clean them at once, Pat. If you are going to walk in all the mud you can find, you can clean them yourself!'

The children stood sulkily in the bedroom. Bother! Blow! They were just going to see Bray.

Auntie Sue knew that. 'You won't see that donkey of yours at all today,' she scolded. 'All you think about is rushing off here, there and everywhere and doing exactly what you like without ever thinking of the trouble you give anyone else. I've a good mind to send you back home.'

This was a terrible threat! Holidaying in the country with dogs and hens and horses, and cows and sheep, and dear old Bray was much better than being in a crowded town. The two children began to clear up at once.

Auntie Sue spoke to Uncle Ben about them. 'I don't know how to make those two pull themselves together and try to remember the things they must do, Ben. They are nice children but so spoilt. They're forgetful and careless, and yet they never get into mischief like some children do.'

'They'll learn one day,' said Uncle Ben. 'Something

will teach them. You'll see!'

'Well, I wish whatever it is would hurry up and come, then,' said Auntie Sue. 'I'm tired of always running round after them.'

The children didn't see Bray that day. He stood by the gate waiting, but they didn't come. He was sad and the children were sadder still. 'We'll go tomorrow,' said Biddy. 'I shall have lots of sugar to take him. Poor Bray. He will be feeling so lonely today.'

They set off to visit him after breakfast the next day. They had remembered to make their beds and put away their things. Bray was waiting for them at the gate. He gave a loud 'He-haw' of welcome.

'He sounds as if he's laughing for joy,' said Pat. 'Good old Bray.'

They were soon petting the old donkey, and then they rode him round the field. They quite forgot the time, and when the church clock struck twelve they slid off Bray's back in horror.

'Twelve o'clock! And Auntie told us to be back by

eleven o'clock sharp to go and do some shopping for her!' They rushed back to the house. Auntie Sue was just beginning to feel cross. Those children!

They had been in such a hurry that they hadn't shut the field gate. They hadn't even shut the garden gate! And they left the kitchen door open behind them, so in walked two hens, a duck and three chicks. Auntie Sue shooed them out and banged the door.

'Why you can't remember even such a simple thing as shutting a door, I don't know,' she said. 'There is the shopping list – there is the basket – and here is the money. Go along before I find myself getting cross with you again, and PLEASE SHUT THE DOOR BEHIND YOU!'

They did. They scurried off to the village at top speed. Oh dear – how difficult it was to remember everything they were told to do!

They did all the shopping and made their way back home. As they drew near they heard some very peculiar sounds. Shouting, yelling, galloping, thuds and crashes!

Gracious, whatever could be happening?

They ran to see – and they stood still in horror and grief. Uncle Ben and two men were hitting Bray, yelling at him, and Bray was cantering madly about the garden, with hens scuttling away from his hoofs.

Pat and Biddy flung down the shopping and rushed to their uncle. 'Don't! Don't! Why are you hitting poor Bray like that? Oh, you're hurting him. DON'T, Uncle, DON'T!'

Bray crashed into a frame of cucumbers and Uncle Ben gave him such a whack with a stick that the donkey leapt into the air with fright. One of the men tried to catch him, but Bray ran the other way, right across the bed of roses that Auntie Sue loved so much. Biff! Uncle Ben hit him again.

Biddy was crying desperately. Pat tried to hang on to his uncle's arm to stop him hitting Bray again, but his uncle, who was in a furious temper, shook him off. 'Get away, you stupid boy! If I don't get this donkey out of here, he'll ruin every flower and vegetable your aunt has grown this year!'

Suddenly Bray ran out of the garden gate and up the lane. One of the farm men chased him. Pat and Biddy wanted to go, too, and comfort Bray, but Uncle Ben took hold of them and led them indoors. They were both crying bitterly. 'You cruel, unkind man!' sobbed Biddy. 'I'll never like you again. I wish you weren't my uncle!'

Auntie Sue stood by the window staring out at her ruined flowers, spoilt lettuces and rows of radishes, and the broken frames. She looked sad.

'That donkey!' raged Uncle Ben. 'I'll get rid of him! I'll sell him tomorrow! Going back to his old tricks again – well, he's had a good thrashing, anyhow!'

'How did he get here?' asked Auntie Sue. 'I suppose his field gate had been left open by some walker or other – and our garden gate must have been left open, too.'

Pat felt his heart suddenly sink down into his boots. The gates! Why, he and Biddy hadn't shut them behind them when they had run off at twelve o'clock in such a hurry. Bray must have got out – and come to look for Biddy and Pat, his friends. And what did he find? Men yelling and shouting at him, men chasing him and hitting him with sticks. And now he would be sold, and have to live in a place he didn't know and with people he probably wouldn't like. Pat gave such a gulp that Biddy looked at him in surprise.

'Uncle! Don't sell Bray! It was our fault – we left the gates open!' he said. 'He came to look for us – he didn't mean to do any damage! I expect he got frightened when you yelled at him, and then he galloped about. Oh, Uncle, please, please don't sell him.'

His uncle looked at him grimly, and then at Biddy. 'So *you* left the gates open – after all you've been told! And because of you the garden is ruined and Bray has been beaten, and may be sold. I hope you feel pleased with yourselves. Careless, spoilt children! Nothing will teach you to pull yourselves together and be a bit responsible. I shall sell Bray tomorrow.'

He got up and went out, still angry. Auntie Sue looked at the two unhappy children sadly. 'I'm afraid Bray *will* be sold,' she said. 'It's dreadful to think he will have to leave his home, when he is so old, all because of you two.' The children couldn't eat any dinner at all. They went out into the ruined garden. Pat began to try and put things straight. 'We'll do what we can,' he said to Biddy. 'We simply must. I feel awful.'

They worked hard for three hours. They rolled the lawn to level out Bray's hoof-marks. They rolled the paths. They raked over the prints he had made in the beds. They tied up broken plants. Pat took all the money out of his money-box to pay for the broken frame. He felt as if he would never smile again.

Auntie Sue must have said something to Uncle Ben about it, because he didn't look nearly so cross at teatime. The children hardly dared to say a word. But at last Pat screwed up enough courage to ask a question.

'When are you going to sell Bray? Please, Uncle, may we come with you and see who you're going to sell him to? We – we want to say goodbye to him, you see. We want to explain things to him.'

'Now, you listen to me,' said Uncle Ben seriously. 'I'm not going to sell Bray, because your aunt tells me you've been trying to put right the damage that has been done because of you – and also because I'm going to give you one more chance. You won't forget in a hurry how horrible it is to see somebody else suffering because of a silly thing *you've* done, will you?'

'Oh, no – we'll never, never forget,' said Biddy, tears coming into her eyes when she thought of poor Bray being hit so hard. 'Uncle, give us another chance. We'll go and tell Bray we're sorry he was hurt, and we'll tell him that because he was hurt we'll never do silly things again.'

'All right!' said her uncle gruffly. 'You can go and see your precious donkey now. And take him this apple from me!'

So off they went as fast as their legs would take them. Do you suppose they kept their word? Well, if a thing like that happened to me, I'd never forget my promise. Nor would you!

Look Out for the Elephant!

Look Out for the Elephant!

'THERE'S AN elephant loose!' shouted Jim, rushing into the school playground. 'I just heard a man say so. It's escaped from the circus.'

'Where is it, where is it?' cried all the children, rushing round Jim.

'It's in the park – and they're afraid it will trample down all the lovely flowers,' said Jim.

'Oh, what a shame!' said Sara. She loved flowers, and she couldn't bear to think of the elephant's great feet trampling and breaking them all.

'They've sent for men with sticks,' said Jim. 'They'll scare that bad elephant properly. I wouldn't mind chasing him myself.'

'But elephants are *nice*,' said Sara. 'I rode on one heaps of times at the zoo. They are gentle and kind. They can't help being big and having enormous feet. I think it's horrid to send for men with sticks!'

'All right, then – *you* go and get the elephant out of the park!' said Jim scornfully. 'Go on! See if it will come and eat out of your hand and follow you like a dog! I tell you, big sticks are the only thing to frighten an elephant!'

Sara stood listening to Jim. She was just about to tell him that an elephant *had* eaten out of her hand at the zoo when she had given him a bun – and then a grand idea came into her head!

Now when Sara had an idea she always acted on it at once. So she turned and ran over to the baker's. She bought twelve buns out of her pocket money and put them into her school satchel.

You can guess what her idea was now, can't you? Well, well – whoever would think of such a thing? Only Sara!

She ran down the street and made for the park. It wasn't very far away. There was a place in the hedge she could get through. She squeezed through it, and there she was in the park. Where was the elephant?

Well, he wasn't very difficult to see, as you can imagine. There he stood, waving his enormous trunk to and fro, his great feet very near to a big bed of glorious dahlias.

In the distance Sara could hear shouting, and she guessed that men were coming with sticks.

'They'll only scare him and he'll go galloping over the dahlias,' thought Sara. 'I'd better hurry.'

So she trotted down the path to where the big elephant stood. She went right up to him.

'You're awfully like the elephant who gave me rides at the zoo,' she told him, and he looked down at her out of little, twinkling eyes. He flapped his ears and made a little trumpeting noise.

'Are you asking for a bun?' said Sara, and she put her hand in her satchel. 'Well, here's one.'

The elephant put out his trunk and took the bun. He swung his trunk up to his big mouth – and the bun was gone! He held out his trunk for another.

'Well, you can have all my buns if you come quietly down this path with me,' said Sara, 'away from these lovely flower-beds. Your feet are so big, you know. Here you are, here's another bun.'

She gave him another, and then began to walk down the path to the park gate. The elephant, seeing that she had plenty more buns, followed her closely, trying to put his trunk inside the satchel.

Sara laughed. 'Oh, you wait until I give you one! There you are. Now do come along. We'll soon be at the gate!'

Well, well, well! The men with sticks stopped at once when they saw the elephant following little Sara like a dog.

'Look at that!' they said. 'That kid has got old Jumbo eating out of her hand! Send his keeper to that park gate – that will be the place to capture the elephant. He's not scared any more, or angry. Well, would you believe it!'

Jumbo followed Sara all the way to the gate, eating the buns she gave him – and there at the gate was the elephant's keeper waiting for him! Jumbo was very glad indeed to see him. He loved his keeper.

'Thank you, little girl,' said the keeper gratefully. 'If it hadn't been for you, poor Jumbo would have been sent racing all over the flower-beds in fright, and he might have done a lot of damage. Now – is there any reward you'd like for getting him to come quietly?'

'Well,' said Sara, 'I suppose – I suppose I couldn't ride on his head, could I, right past our school? The children would hardly believe it if they saw me there!'

'Yes. Old Jumbo will set you on his head and hold you there with his trunk,' said the keeper with a laugh. 'Hup, Jumbo, hup!'

Jumbo picked up Sara very gently and set her on his big head. Then, holding her there with his trunk, he set off down the road that led past the school, swaying this way and that.

'Look! LOOK! It's Sara up there!' shouted the children. 'Hurrah for Sara! Sara, how did you get there? Oh, SARA!'

It was a lovely reward, wasn't it? She deserved it, though, because she really did have a very good idea!

Staying with
Auntie Sue

Staying with Auntie Sue

'WHERE ARE we going to for our holidays this summer, Mummy?' asked Katie. 'I want to go to the seaside again – the same place as last year.'

'Daddy and I are going away by ourselves for a change, dear,' said her mother. 'I feel rather tired, and want to be just with Daddy.'

'But what's to happen to *me*?' cried Katie, in dismay. '*I* want to come too.'

'No, Katie,' said Daddy. 'You're going to stay with your Auntie Sue. You haven't behaved very well lately, and Mummy and I are afraid we've spoilt you. I think it will do Mummy good to leave you with someone else for a little while – you really are growing selfish and rude, you know!'

Katie was quite horrified. She was an only child, and she *had* been spoilt. Mummy was far too easy with her, and now Katie had grown into a most unpleasant little girl.

'I don't like Auntie Sue,' said Katie. 'She doesn't like me either.'

'Oh yes she does,' said her mother, who simply couldn't imagine anyone not liking her beautiful, precious Katie. 'She will be very nice to you indeed.'

So Katie went to stay with Auntie Sue. She wasn't very nice to her aunt. 'I wanted to go with Mummy and Daddy,' she said. 'I didn't want to come and stay with you!'

'Well, I'm afraid you'll have to put up with me, Katie!' said her aunt, cheerfully. 'I hope you'll help me, and will like the things I cook for you.'

But Katie was quite determined she wouldn't help, and wouldn't like anything at all! Making her stay with Auntie Sue when she wanted to go to the seaside!

So she wouldn't run a single errand. She turned up her pretty little nose at treacle pudding and at ginger cake. She even stamped her foot at her aunt. What she really wanted, of course, was a good slap, but Auntie Sue knew that Katie's mother would never forgive her if she slapped her.

'I hope you don't behave like this at home, Katie,' said her aunt. 'I don't wonder your mother needs a holiday without you, if you do. You seem to expect to do everything that you like, and nothing that you don't!'

'That's a good idea,' said Katie. 'I shall go to bed when I like, I shall get up when I like, I shall wear what clothes I like, and I shall *DO* just what I like!'

She expected her auntie to be very upset and cross, and to argue with her. But Auntie Sue gave a little laugh, looked up from her sewing, and said: 'Very well, Katie. I won't bother about you, if you feel like that. Do what you please!'

'Good!' thought Katie. 'That's fine.' So that night she stayed up until ten o'clock. Think of it! Ten o'clock, when all children should have been in bed for a long, long time.

Auntie Sue said nothing at all. At ten she put her book away, said good night to Katie, and went upstairs. Katie thought she would stay up even later, but somehow the house seemed too empty and quiet. So she went up to bed.

In the morning she overslept herself, of course, for she was very tired. She awoke about half-past nine, scrambled into her clothes, and went downstairs to breakfast.

But there wasn't any. 'I've had mine,' said Auntie Sue. 'I always have it at quarter-past eight. I've cleared away and washed up, because I have to go out and do the shopping.'

So Katie had no breakfast, and she was very cross indeed. Auntie Sue went out with her shopping bag. Katie went to the larder. But it was locked! So she couldn't get anything to eat. Bother, bother, bother!

She was very naughty at dinner-time. She ate with her arms on the table, and spilt gravy and fruit-juice down the front of her dress.

'It doesn't matter,' she said. 'I'll put on my best dress this afternoon. Then you can wash this one, Auntie Sue!'

'I shan't have time,' said Auntie Sue. So she didn't wash the dirty dress. Katie put on her best blue velvet one. Then she did something she knew she shouldn't do in her very best dress.

She got out her plasticine and her paint-box and began playing with them. 'You know you have an overall, don't you?' said Auntie Sue.

'Course I do,' said Katie, 'but I want to play like this.' When teatime came you should have seen Katie's dress! It was splashed with paint, and had marks all over it where she had wiped the plasticine off her fingers. It was quite spoilt.

Auntie Sue called her to tea. 'I can't come till I've

finished my picture,' answered Katie rudely.

And, oh dear, when at last she did go to tea, that was all cleared away too, just as breakfast had been. Katie stamped and yelled, but Auntie Sue took no notice.

'You do what you like, and there is no reason why I should not do the same,' she said, sewing quietly. 'Stop shouting or you will upset Tinker.'

Tinker was the cat. He didn't like Katie at all, because she pulled his tail. Katie gave another terrific yell, and Tinker flew at her. He dug his claws into her arm, and gave her a line of red scratches. Then Katie yelled in earnest.

'Tinker is going to do what *he* likes too,' said Auntie Sue. 'You'd better bathe your arm. It isn't very nice, is it, Katie, when we do what we like, and don't bother about one another? But you have chosen that way of behaving, and I will choose it too. So will Tinker.'

At half-past six Auntie Sue looked at the clock. 'Will you go and turn on the gas under the little saucepan in the kitchen?' she said.

'No,' said Katie, who wasn't going to do a single thing if she could help it. Auntie Sue said nothing. She didn't go out to the kitchen to turn on the gas either.

'I'm hungry,' said Katie at last. 'I've had no tea. I want something to eat.'

'Well, I did tell you to turn on the gas under the little saucepan in the kitchen,' said Auntie Sue. 'I was going to cook you an egg. But I shan't bother now, as *you* didn't bother.'

'I will bother, I will!' said Katie, suddenly feeling hungry enough to eat a dozen eggs. She flew out to the kitchen and lit the gas.

She boiled the egg herself, cut some bread and butter, and had it for her supper. Then she actually went up to bed. But her bed was not made, and the room was dusty and untidy.

She rushed downstairs. 'Auntie Sue! You forgot to make my bed! And my room's terrible.'

'Put it right, then,' said Auntie Sue. 'And if you

want your bed made, make it yourself. I am doing what I like, remember, just as you are – and I *don't* like making your bed or doing your room.'

Katie was angry and shouted. But Auntie Sue took no notice. Tinker suddenly stood up – and Katie fled. She wasn't going to be scratched by that horrid, bad-tempered cat again!

She was down to breakfast in good time the next morning. She had on another clean dress, her last clean one, for she had only brought three with her.

'Hadn't you better put on your overall, as that is your last clean dress?' asked Auntie Sue. '*I* don't mind, of course, but you might possibly want a clean dress some time.'

'I don't like my overall,' said Katie, 'and I don't *want* to put it on.'

And at breakfast-time what did she do but spill her cocoa all down the front of her clean dress!

Auntie Sue didn't say a word. Katie dried her dress as best she could. She rather wished she *had*

had on her overall, but she wasn't going to say so. Oh, dear me, no!

That afternoon the little girl next door came to say she was having a small party, and would Auntie Sue's niece Katie like to come too?

'Oh *yes*,' said Katie. 'I *love* parties!'

When the little girl had gone, Katie spoke to her aunt in rather a meek voice. 'Auntie, all my dresses are dirty. I do like to look nice when I go to a party. Will you wash one for me?'

'I shall have my sewing-meeting here today,' said Auntie Sue. 'I shall have no time.'

'But, Auntie – I can't go to a party in a dirty dress!' said Katie, almost in tears.

'No, you can't possibly,' Auntie agreed. 'You could go in your overall. You haven't worn it, so it's still clean.'

'I *can't* go to a party in an overall!' cried Katie, horrified. 'I can't. Everyone would laugh at me.'

'It might do you good to be laughed at,' said Auntie

Sue. 'Maybe you wouldn't be so careless with your dresses then. Well, do as you like. Wear your overall and go – or don't wear it, and stay at home.'

Katie didn't go, and she sat listening sulkily to all the fun going on next door. She didn't even like to go to see her auntie's sewing friends, because her dress was so dirty. So she went without her tea.

It wasn't much fun doing exactly as she liked if Auntie did the same. Katie was bored, so she made her bed and tidied her room. She felt pleased when she saw how nice it looked. She thought she would go out into the garden and get a few flowers to put in her room. Auntie had said she might, but she hadn't bothered to.

She went out and picked some. Then she picked some for her aunt's bedroom, too! She didn't know why she did, except that she felt she would rather like to have a word of praise from Auntie Sue. It was horrid living with somebody who didn't seem a bit interested in you.

Auntie Sue was very pleased with the flowers. 'That was nice of you, Katie,' she said. 'Now you make me feel *I* want to be nice too. I shall buy tickets for the circus the day after tomorrow!'

But the next day Katie was silly again. She thought she would go for a walk, and off she set, without coat or hat or scarf. Auntie Sue called after her. 'It's going to rain. Wouldn't it be best to wear your mackintosh, sou'wester and rubber boots?'

'Don't fuss, Auntie,' said Katie, cheekily, and wouldn't go back. So, of course, she got caught in a real storm and was soon wet through. She tried to shelter under a tree, but the wind caught her there, and she shivered with cold.

She ran all the way home in the rain. 'You had better get straight into a warm bed,' said Auntie Sue, 'or you will get a cold.'

But Katie wouldn't. She didn't want to. So by the next morning she had a terrible cold and didn't feel well enough to get out of bed at all.

She wondered if Auntie Sue would think she was oversleeping, and clear away the breakfast things again and go out shopping and leave her. Oh dear, and she felt so bad! It would be nice to have somebody being kind to her. She wouldn't be able to go to the circus now, either! Katie cried into her pillow and felt very sorry for herself.

Auntie Sue came in with a breakfast tray. She straightened the bedclothes, banged the pillows, gave Katie two hankies, brushed her hair, and then set the tray in front of her.

'We can't go to the circus,' said Katie, in a small voice. 'I've got such a bad cold. Will the tickets be wasted?'

'My dear child, when I saw you going out yesterday without a mack I knew you would get wet through and have a cold today, so I was not foolish enough to buy the tickets,' said Auntie Sue. 'Now, if you are going to be sensible and do what you are told, for once, then I shall be sensible and kind, too.'

'Oh, I *do* want you to be kind to me today,' begged Katie, and she actually took her aunt's hand. 'I've been awfully silly.'

'You've been worse than silly,' said Auntie Sue, briskly. 'You've been horrible. But there – it's not altogether your fault, as I've said before. You've been spoilt!'

Katie did everything she was told. She ate what her aunt brought her, she took her medicines, she had a sleep in the afternoon, and she was patient and grateful and polite.

'Well!' said Auntie Sue, after tea, opening a book to read to Katie. 'What a surprise you are, Katie! I'd no idea you had any niceness in you. If I'm not careful I shall end up by liking you very much.'

'Oh, do, Auntie!' said Katie. 'I *want* you to like me. I'd be proud if you did. I know I'm spoilt, but I'll try not to be with you. I shan't do what I like any more – I'll do what *you* like!'

'We'll *both* do that,' said Auntie Sue, pleased,

and she opened the book to read to Katie.

She and Katie had a nice time after that – but I don't know what will happen when Katie goes back home to her mother and father. If they spoil her again, it will be hard for her to be nice, won't it? She'd better go and live with Auntie Sue!

A Puppy in Wonderland

A Puppy in Wonderland

CHIPS WAS a round, fat little puppy. He belonged to Alan, James and Kate, and they were all very fond of him. He was rather naughty, because he would chew slippers up, and dig great holes in the garden.

'He's a dear little pup,' said Alan, 'but I do wish he'd stop digging in the garden. Daddy is getting so cross!'

'Let's take him for a walk,' said Kate. 'If we make him tired out, he will go to sleep in his basket, and won't get into any more mischief.'

So they called Chips, and he came bounding up to them, delighted to think that he was going for a walk.

'Where shall we go?' asked Alan.

'Through Heyho Wood,' said James. 'It's such a hot day, and it will be nice and cool there.'

So off they started. It was hot! The sun shone down, and there was not a cloud in the sky. They were glad to get into the shady wood.

Chips ran here and there, sniffing at the ground in great excitement. He could smell rabbits! Then he saw one! Oh, my goodness, what a to-do there was! He yelped and barked, and tore off as fast as his short legs would let him, tripping and tumbling over blackberry brambles as he went!

'Chips! Chips! Come here, you'll get lost!' cried Alan.

But Chips took no notice at all. On he went, bounding through the trees, his little tail wagging like mad. He must catch that rabbit, he really must!

But of course he didn't! The rabbit went diving headlong into its hole, and when Chips came up and looked round there was no rabbit to be seen!

'It must have gone into the ground like worms do!' thought the puppy. So he chose a nice green place, and began to dig. He scrabbled the earth with his front paws, and sent it flying out behind him with his back ones. He puffed and panted, snorted and sneezed, and he took no notice at all of the shouts and whistles of the children some distance away.

Suddenly there came a shout of rage. Chips looked up in surprise, and what did he see but a brownie, dressed in a brown tunic, long stockings and a pointed hat! He was staring at Chips with a very angry look on his face, and the puppy wondered why. He didn't wonder long, because he suddenly remembered the rabbit again, and once more began to dig madly.

That made the brownie crosser than ever. He took a long green whistle from his pocket and blew seven short blasts on it. Immediately a crowd of little men like himself came up.

'Look!' said the first brownie, fiercely. 'Look at that horrid dog! He's dug a hole right in the very middle of the fairy ring which we got ready for the Queen's dance tonight! And he won't stop, either!'

'Stop! Stop, you naughty dog!' cried all the brownies. 'Stop digging at once!'

But Chips took no notice at all. He just went on digging. The brownies didn't know what to do.

'He may bite if we go too near him,' said one. 'But we must catch him and punish him. Why, the Queen won't be able to have her midnight dance tonight!'

'I know how we can get him!' cried a small brownie. 'Let's go and ask the spiders to give us some of their web! Then we'll throw it round the dog and catch him like that!'

'That's a good idea!' cried all the little men. 'Then we'll take him to prison.'

Chips looked up. He thought the brownies looked very cross indeed. He decided that he would go and find the children. But the brownies had closed round him in a ring, and he could see no way to get through. Then two or three of them came running up with a large net made of sticky spider thread. They suddenly threw it over the puppy – and poor Chips was caught!

He tried to get out of the web, but he couldn't. The brownies dragged him away, and he yelped miserably. The children heard him yelping, and looked at one another.

'Chips is in trouble!' said Kate. 'Quick, come and see what's the matter!'

The three children ran as fast as they could to where they heard the puppy yelping. But when they got there, there was no Chips to be seen. There was only a cross-looking brownie filling in a newly-dug hole.

'Oh!' said the children in surprise, and stopped to look at the funny little man. He looked at them, too, and then went on with his work.

'I suppose you haven't seen our puppy, have you?' asked Kate, at last.

'Oh, so it was your dog, was it?' said the brownie. 'Well, do you know what he has done? Do you see this ring of fine green grass, surrounded by toadstools? It was made ready for a dance tonight, by order of the Queen – and your horrid little dog dug a great big hole in the middle of it. It's all spoilt!'

'Oh dear, I am sorry,' said Alan. 'He really is naughty to do that – but I'm sure he didn't mean any harm. He's only a puppy, you know. He's not four months old yet.'

'Well, he's been taken to prison,' said the brownie. 'He wouldn't even stop when we told him to!'

Kate began to cry. She couldn't bear to think of poor little Chips being taken to prison. Alan put his arm round her.

'Don't worry, Kate,' he said. 'We'll find some way of rescuing him.'

The brownie laughed.

'Oh, no, you won't!' he said. 'We shan't set him free until he's sorry.'

He ran off, and disappeared between the trees. The children stared at one another in dismay.

'We must find Chips!' said Kate. 'Where can they have put him?'

'Look, here are the marks of their footsteps,' said James pointing to where the grass was trodden down. 'Let's follow their tracks as far as we can.'

So they set off. Chips had been carried by the brownies, so they could find no marks of his toes, but they could easily follow the traces left on the long grass by the crowd of brownies.

Through the trees they went, keeping their eyes on the ground. Suddenly the tracks stopped.

'That's funny!' said Alan. 'Where can they all have gone to? Look! They stop quite suddenly just here, in the middle of this little clearing.'

'Perhaps they've flown into the air,' suggested Kate.

'I don't think so,' said Alan. 'That little fellow we met had no wings.'

'Well, did they go down through the ground then?' wondered James. He looked hard at the grass, and then gave a cry of excitement.

'Look!' he said, 'I do believe there's a trap-door here, with grass growing neatly all over it!'

The children looked down – yes, James was right. There was a square patch there, which might well be a trap-door.

Alan knelt down, and after a few minutes he found out how to lift up the trap-door. James and Kate looked down the opening in excitement. They saw a tiny flight of steps leading into darkness. Alan took out his torch and flashed it into the hole.

'Look!' he cried, and picked up a white hair. 'Here's one of Chips's hairs. Now we know they took him down this way! Come on!'

The three children scrambled down. There were twenty steps, and then a stone platform. To their great astonishment they saw an underground river flowing by.

'Well, Chips must have gone this way because there's no other way for him to go!' said James. 'But how are we to follow? There's no boat to take us.'

But just at that moment a little blue boat floated up, and came to the platform, where it stayed quite still.

'Hurrah!' said Alan. 'Here's just what we want. Come on, you two.'

They all jumped in at once, and the little boat floated away down the dark stream. After a while it came out into the open air, and the children were very glad.

They looked round them in wonder.

'This must be Wonderland!' said Kate. 'Look at all the beautiful castles and palaces!'

'And look at the funny higgledy-piggledy cottages everywhere!' said James.

'And what a crowd of different kinds of fairyfolk!' said Alan. 'Look, brownies, elves, pixies, gnomes, and lots of others!'

'I wonder where the brownies took Chips,' said Kate. 'Shall we ask someone and see if they know?'

'Yes,' said Alan. So they stopped the boat by

guiding it gently to the bank, and then asked a passing pixie if he had seen any brownies with a puppy.

'Yes,' he said. 'They had him wrapped up in a spider's web, and took him to that castle over there.'

He pointed to a castle nearby on a steep hill.

'Thank you,' said Alan. Then he turned to the others. 'Come on,' he said. 'We must leave this boat, and make for the castle.'

Out they jumped, and took the path that led to the castle. It was not long before they were climbing the hill on which the castle stood. They came to a great gate, and by it hung a bellrope.

Alan pulled it, and at once a jangling noise was heard in the courtyard beyond. The gate swung open, and the children went in, feeling a little bit frightened.

There was no one in the courtyard. Exactly opposite was a door, which stood open. The children went towards it and peeped inside. Just as they got there they heard a sorrowful bark.

'Chips is here!' said Kate, in a whisper. 'Let's go in.'

They crept inside the door, and found themselves in a big hall. At one end was a raised platform on which stood a very grand chair, almost a throne. On it was sitting a very solemn brownie. In front of him, still tied up in the spider's thread, was poor Chips, very much afraid. Round him were scores of little brownies, and they were telling the chief one what he had done.

Kate ran right up to the solemn brownie, and James and Alan followed.

'Please, please let our puppy go!' begged Kate. 'He didn't mean any harm to your fairy ring. He was after a rabbit, that's all.'

'What sort of rabbit?' asked the chief brownie.

'Oh, a big sandy one, with white tips to its ears,' said Alan. 'I saw it just as it ran away from Chips.'

'Then he's a good puppy, not a naughty one!' cried the solemn brownie. 'That rabbit is very bad. It used to pull the Queen's carriage, and what do you think it did?'

'What?' asked the three children.

'Why, one night, it ran away with the carriage!' said the brownie. 'The poor Queen was so frightened. The carriage turned over, and she was thrown out. The rabbit ran off, and we have never been able to catch it since.'

'Well, Chips nearly caught it!' said Kate, eagerly. 'And I expect he saw it go into a burrow, and tried to dig it out – only he chose the wrong place, that's all. I'm sure he's very sorry indeed for all the trouble he has caused.'

'Wuff-wuff! Wuff-wuff!' said Chips, sitting up on his back legs, and begging for mercy.

'We'll let him go at once!' cried all the brownies, and two of them ran to cut away the web that bound him. In no time at all Chips was free, and danced delightedly round the three children. Kate picked him up and hugged him.

'Take them back to the wood,' commanded the chief brownie. 'And give Chips a bone to make up for his fright.'

The puppy barked in glee when a large bone was given to him. He picked it up in his mouth and began to chew it.

'The carriage is at the door,' said a little brownie, running in. The children were taken to the great door, and outside in the yard stood a grand carriage of silver and gold, driven by a brownie driver. Six small white horses drew the carriage. How excited the children were!

They all got in, said goodbye to the brownies, and then off went the carriage at a smart pace. It went up hill and down dale, through miles of Wonderland, and at last entered the same wood in which their adventures had started that morning.

'Thank you so much,' said the children as they jumped out. They patted the horses, and then the carriage turned round and was soon out of sight.

The children walked home, and told their mother all that had happened. But she found it very difficult to believe them.

'Are you sure you haven't made it all up?' she asked.

'Well, look, here is the bone that the brownies gave to Chips!' cried Kate. 'And look at his tail! It's still covered with spider's web!'

So it was – and after that their mother had to believe their exciting story, especially as Chips had learnt his lesson, and never, never, never, dug a hole in the garden again!

The Three Sailors

The Three Sailors

PETER, ROSEMARY and Richard were staying by the sea. Their house was almost on the beach. It was lovely. Every day they had tea on the beach, and Granny, Mummy and Daddy came too.

Granny didn't like sitting on the sand, so Daddy had brought down a chair and a wooden table from the house for her. Mummy had a tablecloth, and Granny sat up to the table and poured out tea and milk for everyone.

After tea the children wanted to go out in a boat.

'No,' said Daddy. 'Not today. I want to finish my book. Besides, the sea is too rough today. You wouldn't like going in a boat.'

'Oh, Daddy, we should, we should!' said Peter. 'We are such good sailors. Can't we go in a boat by ourselves? We could manage it quite all right.'

'Certainly not!' said Daddy.

So the three children had to be good and dig castles in the sand. Granny helped them. She gave them bits of coloured wool too, to put among the seaweed for flowers when they made a garden for the castle.

'Perhaps Daddy will take you in a boat tomorrow,' she said.

The next day the sea was just as rough, but the children ran to ask their father to get a boat.

'No, the sea is still too rough,' Daddy said. 'You might be sea-sick.'

'Oh, Daddy, we wouldn't be, really and truly!' said Richard. 'We are such good sailors. Do take us! Oh, do get a boat and let us go out in it!'

But Daddy wouldn't. He said they could none

of them swim well enough to go out in a boat on a rough sea.

'I'm sure I could swim all right if I fell out of a boat,' said Rosemary, sulking.

Then Daddy got cross and said nobody was to mention boats again till he did. So the three children set to work to dig, though they all looked rather sulky.

It was Granny who thought of a good idea for them. 'Why don't you turn the wooden table upside down and pretend it's a boat?' she said. 'That would be fun. You could tie the tablecloth to Daddy's stick and tie that to one of the table legs, and you would have a mast and sail. Your spades can be oars.'

'Oooh, yes! We'll play pirates!' cried Richard in excitement. 'Come and help, you others.'

The table was quickly turned upside down, and Richard began to tie Daddy's stick to a leg for a mast. Then Rosemary tied the tablecloth to the stick, and the wind flapped it out for a fine sail. It was most exciting!

'Daddy and Granny and I are going for a walk this afternoon till tea-time,' said Mummy. 'We will bring tea down with us when we come back. Amuse yourselves well and have a nice afternoon, all of you.'

The three children were left on the beach alone. They were pleased. Now they could play pirates and shout all they wanted to. What a fine boat the big wooden table made!

They got the cushions out of the chairs in the house and put them in the upside-down table. They got their spades for oars. The sail flapped merrily in the breeze.

'Yo-ho for a life on the ocean wave!' shouted Peter. 'We'll have some fine adventures!'

They did! They sailed after ships and caught them. They took prisoners. They had a wreck. They did enjoy their game, and at last they were so hot and tired that they didn't want to play any more.

'I'm going to have a rest,' said Peter, flopping down on a cushion in the upside-down table.

'So am I,' said Rosemary, fanning herself.

'Let's pretend that we are drifting off to a wonderful treasure island!' said Richard. 'Ship your oars, everyone! While we rest, our ship will take us to a wonderful land where we can find hidden treasure.'

They all lay down on the cushions and shut their eyes. The sun shone down. It was lovely and hot. The little breeze cooled them nicely. In two minutes all three children were fast asleep.

Now the tide was coming in very fast, with the wind behind it. A big wave ran right up the beach and lapped against the table. The children didn't see it. They were fast asleep, of course. Another wave came, and another. Each one ran up to the table. A bigger wave still ran all round it.

Then such a big wave came that it lifted the table up! Then two more waves ran underneath and took that upside-down table and floated it gently out to sea.

Richard's feet were in the water but he didn't notice it. Rosemary's hair hung over the side of the table and got wet, but she was fast asleep. Peter's spade floated off by itself.

The sea was pleased with its boat. It bobbed it up and down, up and down – and suddenly a wave splashed right over the table and woke all three children up with a jump!

They sat up in a hurry. How astonished they were to find themselves out at sea on their table! The beach looked a long, long way away.

'Oooh! Our table's a real boat!' said Peter, looking scared.

'The sea has taken it away!' said Rosemary.

'We wanted to go out in a boat by ourselves and now we have,' said Richard, not liking it at all.

'I feel sick,' said Peter, holding on to the table, for it was bobbing up and down tremendously on the waves.

'So do I,' said Rosemary.

'I feel frightened,' said Richard, beginning to cry. 'We can't swim enough to save ourselves.'

'I told Daddy I could, but I daren't,' said Rosemary.

'Oh, what shall we do?' cried Richard. 'I'm scared!'

The three poor sailors clung to the bobbing table for all they were worth. The tablecloth sail flapped merrily. The cushions were soaked every time a big wave broke on the table.

'We shall be drowned!' said Peter, looking very white.

'If only someone would rescue us!' cried Richard, his tears tasting as salt as the sea-spray.

'Look! There's Daddy coming down to the beach with the tea things!' said Rosemary.

'Yell as loud as you can,' said Peter.

So they yelled, 'Dad-dee, Dad-dee, Dad-dee!'

Their father was looking round the beach in surprise, seeing no children. Then he suddenly heard their voices and looked out to sea. How astonished he was to see the three sailors on the table!

'Save us, Daddy, save us!' shouted Peter.

Do you know what Daddy did? He began to laugh and laugh and laugh.

'So you are three sailors after all!' he shouted. 'How do you like it?'

'Oh, Daddy, save us!' shouted Rosemary.

'You silly children, jump into the water and wade to shore with the table!' yelled Daddy.

'Daddy, we shall be drowned!' wept Richard. 'The sea is so deep!'

'Peter! Jump out and wade to shore!' shouted Daddy again. 'Go on, do as I tell you. I'm not going to wet my nice white trousers to come and fetch you in.'

Peter put one leg over the table into the sea. He clung hard to the table-leg and let himself go into the water. Splash!

What a surprise for him! Although he was so far out from shore the sea was only up to his knees. It took a long time for the sea to get really deep there, for the tide flowed in over level sand.

'Oh! We can paddle back,' said Peter in surprise.

'I'm only up to my knees. Get out, Rosemary, and help.'

Rosemary jumped out. Then Richard jumped too, and together the three sailors paddled back to the beach, dragging their table behind them.

'Well, well, well!' said Daddy, still laughing. 'Who's going to worry me to take them out in a boat on a rough sea again?'

Nobody said a word. Nobody wanted to go out in a boat on the rough sea now. The three sailors were rather ashamed of themselves. But Granny and Mummy were quite excited to hear about the adventure, so they all cheered up, put the table the right way up for Granny, and had a lovely tea.

The Magic Seaweed

The Magic Seaweed

ONE DAY Jill was building a sandcastle by the sea. It was a lovely one with passages here and there through it, and a proper tower at the top with windows to look through, and a nice courtyard paved with little white stones.

All round the castle was a moat that Jill had dug herself. She fetched some water from the sea to fill it, but the water sank down through the sand and the moat stayed dry.

'Never mind!' said her mother, who was sitting near by, reading. 'When the tide comes in, it will fill your moat and then the castle will look lovely, all surrounded by blue water!'

Jill finished the castle and then sat down to wait for the tide. She picked up a bit of red seaweed lying on the sand near her and began to pop the little bladders in it, one by one.

Suddenly she came to an oddly-shaped little bladder, and she popped it just as she had done the others – and inside she found a little pink sweet! Jill looked at it in astonishment.

It certainly looked like a sweet – but did it taste like one? Jill popped it into her mouth to see. Yes, it was lovely and sweet and tasted of strawberries!

The little girl sucked till it was gone – and then she saw that a very strange thing had happened. She had grown quite small! She wasn't even as tall as her little pail lying near by!

'Goodness, that seaweed must be magic!' said Jill. 'I've gone small. Oh my, doesn't Mummy look big! She's just like a giantess!'

Jill looked at her sandcastle. It looked very, very

big to her now, and she thought she would like to explore it. She ran across the dry moat and climbed up the little sandy steps she had made in the side of the castle and went inside.

It was all very exciting. She ran down one of the passages, and was surprised to hear someone speaking to her.

'Hello, pixie! Where did you come from?'

Jill turned and saw a crab as big as herself. She felt a little bit afraid at first, but the crab looked at her kindly, and she thought that he looked too nice to nip her.

'I'm not a pixie,' she said. 'I'm just a little girl gone very small. I ate a magic sweet out of one of those bladders in the seaweed.'

'Dear me, that's very interesting,' said the crab, crawling out of the damp corner he was hiding in. 'Have you come to live here?'

'Oh no,' said Jill. 'I've only come to explore. I built this castle when I was big, you know.'

'Very clever of you,' said the crab. 'But how are you going to get out again? The tide is coming in, and soon the castle will be surrounded by water!'

'Oh, goodness me, I'd better go quickly then,' said Jill, in a fright. 'I never thought of that.'

She turned and ran down the passage to the sandy steps that led to the moat. But when she got to the moat she stood still and stared.

A big wave had swept up the sand and had filled the moat all round the castle! Water rippled against the sandy walls, and now that Jill was so tiny, she knew she could not possibly wade through it. It was much too deep!

'Whatever shall I do?' she said. 'Perhaps Mummy will hear me if I shout, and lift me off.'

So she shouted to her mother at the top of her voice. But Mother didn't hear at all. The sea was making such a noise and Jill's voice was now so small that she could hardly hear it herself!

'Well, Mummy can't hear me, that's certain,' said

Jill. 'I'll go back to the crab and see what he's going to do. He's here too.'

So she went back to him and asked him.

'That's easy,' said the crab. 'I shall wait until the castle crumbles right away into the sea and then swim down to the sandy bottom and bury myself there! Why don't you do the same?'

'Little girls don't do things like that,' said Jill. 'Oh dear, whatever shall I do? Look, there's another big wave gone by and filled the moat up again. And, oh dear, it has washed away my nice sandy steps up to this passage. Perhaps the next one will come into this very passage, Mister Crab! I'm going up to the top of the castle. I shall feel safer there!'

She ran out of the passage and climbed up the side of the castle till she came to the little doorway she had made in the castle walls at the top. She slipped through it and found herself in the courtyard of white pebbles. They seemed very big to her now. She ran to a window and looked out. Oh my goodness, the sea was certainly coming in fast!

'It will be all round the castle in a minute!' she thought. 'Look at that enormous wave!'

Smack! The wave broke just near the castle, and the sea ran all round it. There was no moat to be seen now, for the tide had quite surrounded the castle. Jill could see nothing but green sea all around.

Smack! Another big wave broke, and Jill felt the castle shake beneath her.

'The castle will soon be gone,' said the crab, suddenly appearing through the doorway. 'It doesn't take long for the sea to destroy a building made of sand, you know.'

'But this is dreadful!' cried Jill, in a great fright. 'Why, I might be drowned! Oh, do look at the next wave!'

Smack! The wave broke so far up the castle that all the front side of it crumbled down into the sea! Only the back of it stood above the water, and poor Jill clambered to the very highest piece. Oh dear! What a tiny island she was on, and what a big sea was all around her! Her mother had moved further up the beach, out of the reach of the water. She didn't seem to miss Jill at all.

'Mummy! Mummy!' called Jill, in a tiny voice. 'Do take off your shoes and rescue me! I shall be drowned!'

But of course her mother couldn't hear anything, with the waves making such a noise.

'Well, little girl, I expect the next few waves will smash the castle to pieces,' said the crab, poking a leg out of the sand in which he had been burying himself. 'I'll say goodbye, I think.'

'Oh, don't go!' cried Jill. 'I'm frightened!'

But he was gone, and Jill saw him no more on the castle. She looked out to sea. Oh, what big waves there were! The poor castle shivered and shook beneath them, and each time one broke the castle slid further down into the sea. Soon there was only a small tip of sand left.

Jill looked up the beach at her mother in despair.

She saw that Mother had suddenly missed her. She was looking everywhere for her, and calling her.

'Jill! Jill! Come here!' she cried. But Jill couldn't come. And at that very moment the biggest wave of all came along and swept right over the top of the castle. It took Jill along with it, and she gasped and spluttered in fright.

Then she heard Mother's voice again:

'Jill! Jill! Wake up, do! The waves are all over your feet, you silly child!'

Jill opened her eyes – and dear me, what a very peculiar thing! She was lying on the beach by her sandcastle, and the tide was coming in. A great big wave had broken near it and had run round her feet!

'Why, I must have been asleep and dreamed it all!' said Jill, in astonishment. 'Fancy that! But goodness me, what a good thing it was only a dream! I was really getting quite afraid. All right, Mummy, I'm coming. I was dreaming.'

Just at that moment a tiny crab looked up out of

the wet sand beside her. It was such a knowing little creature that Jill felt sure it was the one that had been on the castle with her.

'Perhaps it wasn't a dream after all,' she said. 'But it must have been, because there is my castle, still standing!'

'Wouldn't you like to stand on the castle you've made, till the sea is all round it?' asked Mother.

'No, thank you,' said Jill, and her mother couldn't think why she didn't want to. But I can guess why, can't you?

Acknowledgements

All efforts have been made to seek necessary permissions.

The stories in this publication first appeared in the following publications:

At Seaside Cottage was first published as a standalone book by the Brockhampton Press in 1947.

'The Magic Ice Cream' first appeared in *Enid Blyton's Sunny Stories*, issue 222, 1935.

'Wagger Goes to the Show' first appeared in *Enid Blyton's Sunny Stories*, issue 407, 1947.

'A Surprise for Jimmy' first appeared in *Sunny Stories for Little Folks*, issue 163, 1933.

'The Twins Get in a Fix' first appeared in *Enid Blyton's Sunny Stories*, issue 138, 1939.

'The Enchanted Cloak' first appeared in *Enid Blyton's Sunny Stories*, issue 244, 1941.

'Adventure Up a Tree' first appeared in *Enid Blyton's Sunny Stories*, issue 486, 1950.

'John's Hanky' first appeared in *Good Housekeeping*, Jul 1947.

'The Magic Watering Can' first appeared in *Sunny Stories for Little Folks*, issue 227, 1935.

'Peppermint Rock' first appeared in *Enid Blyton's Sunny Stories*, issue 468, 1949.

'The Donkey on the Sands' first appeared in *Enid Blyton's Sunny Stories*, issue 192, 1940.

'In the Middle of the Night' first appeared in *Sunny Stories for Little Folks*, issue 245, 1936.

'A Bit of Blue Sky' first appeared in *Enid Blyton's Sunny Stories*, issue 150, 1939.

'The Smugglers' Caves' first appeared in *Enid Blyton's Sunny Stories*, issue 386, 1946.

'Mr Gobo's Green Grass' first appeared in *Enid Blyton's Sunny Stories*, issue 179, 1940.

'Smokey and the Seagull' first appeared in *Enid Blyton's Magazine*, issue 15, Vol. 4, 1956.

'Adventures Under the Sea' first appeared in *Merry Moments Annual 1923*.

'An Exciting Afternoon' first appeared in *Enid Blyton's Sunny Stories*, issue 417, 1947.

'Lazy Lenny' first appeared as 'Lazy Leonard' in *Enid Blyton's Sunny Stories*, issue 310, 1943.

'Pink Paint for a Pixie' first appeared in *Enid Blyton's Sunny Stories*, issue 303, 1943.

'Shut the Gate' first appeared in *Enid Blyton's Sunny Stories*, issue 424, 1948.

ACKNOWLEDGEMENTS

'Look Out for the Elephant!' first appeared in *Enid Blyton's Sunny Stories*, issue 465, 1949.

'Staying with Auntie Sue' first appeared as 'The Spoilt Little Girl' in *Enid Blyton's Sunny Stories*, issue 399, 1947.

'A Puppy in Wonderland' first appeared as 'A Puppy in Fairyland' in *Sunny Stories for Little Folks*, issue 95, 1930.

'The Three Sailors' first appeared in *Enid Blyton's Sunny Stories*, issue 82, 1938.

'The Magic Seaweed' first appeared in *Sunny Stories for Little Folks*, issue 144, 1932.

More classic stories from the world of

Enid Blyton

The Secret Seven

Join Peter, Janet, Jack, Barbara, Pam, Colin, George
and Scamper as they solve puzzles and mysteries,
foil baddies, and rescue people from danger – all without
help from the grown-ups. Enid Blyton wrote fifteen
stories about the Secret Seven. These editions contain
brilliant illustrations by Tony Ross, plus extra
fun facts and stories to read and share.

More classic stories from the world of

Enid Blyton

The Naughtiest Girl

Elizabeth Allen is spoilt and selfish. When she's sent away to boarding school she makes up her mind to be the naughtiest pupil there's ever been! But Elizabeth soon finds out that being bad isn't as simple as it seems. Thre are ten brilliant books about the Naughtiest Girl to enjoy.

More classic stories from the world of

Enid Blyton

The Famous Five Colour Short Stories

Enid Blyton also wrote eight short stories about the Famous Five. Here they are, in their original texts, with brand-new illustrations. They're a perfect introduction to the gang, and an exciting new way to enjoy classic Blyton stories.

More classic stories from the world of

Enid Blyton

Enid Blyton's Adventure Treasury

A must for Blyton fans, this beautiful giftbook is a
collection of her most exciting writing. Join many of
her best-loved heroes as they solve mysteries,
explore new places and foil baddies!

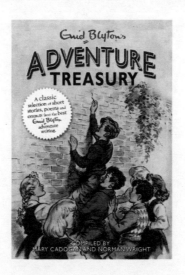